EXPOSED FURY

Marie Flanigan

Exposed Fury
Red Adept Publishing, LLC
104 Bugenfield Court
Garner, NC 27529
http://RedAdeptPublishing.com/

For my husband, Colin Flanigan, without whom none of this would be possible.

CHAPTER ONE
Mid-December, Friday

If not for Chester, Annie wouldn't have noticed the body. A cold wind was stirring when Chester started to bark. Annie tried to keep her footing on the icy pavement as her little white dog strained at his leash, fixated on one of the businesses backed up to the alley. A leg was awkwardly draped over a low brick wall around the back patio as though someone were attempting to climb it, but the leg was covered in snow.

Annie had been enjoying their early-morning walk despite the weather. What had started out as a brief ice storm late last night had then dumped four inches of snow. It was still coming down, giving the historic district of Leesburg, Virginia, a Currier-and-Ives feel, especially with Christmas wreaths on the doors of the shops and candles in many of the windows.

But at the sight of the body, all Annie's winter-wonderland delight fell away. She went into cop mode, picking up Chester and stepping in for a closer look.

The man was facedown with drifting snow covering his upper body. Without thinking, Annie pulled out her cell phone and called her old partner.

"Annie?" Gunnar sounded surprised to be hearing from her. They hadn't talked in a while.

"Hey, Gunnar, sorry to be calling so early, but I was walking my dog, and we found a dead man in the alley next to the town garage."

"What? Did you call it in?" His voice was deep and rough, as though she'd woken him.

"I called you." She regretted it the moment she said it.

"Annie..." He said in a nurturing tone.

It annoyed her. "I know. I'll call nine one one." She used her cop voice, wanting him to know that she wasn't fragile and could handle the situation.

Gunnar responded in kind. "What's it look like?"

"Not sure. He's a big guy, but he's covered in snow. Can you get over here?"

"I'm on my way."

Annie hung up, called 911, and gave the dispatcher the same information she'd given Gunnar. Still holding a squirming Chester, she looked at the body again. The wind had blown some of the snow off his leg to reveal charcoal-gray dress pants, nice socks, and expensive-looking black leather shoes. She looked all around the broad alley, which stretched the block from Loudoun Street to West Market. A pristine blanket of snow covered the whole area. The only footprints were hers and Chester's. She carefully retraced her steps, but balancing on the slick pavement wasn't easy. The back entrance to Leesburg Beer Company was filled with blown snow, and the outdoor seating area behind King's Court Tavern was shuttered for the winter. Nothing looked amiss. The shops and restaurants weren't open yet, and everything was still beneath the blanket of white. She took the steps up to the parking garage's ground floor and stood just inside, out of the wind.

She kept Chester in her arms as he licked her chin and she rubbed his head. As a cop, she'd witnessed her fair share of bodies, but this was the first one she'd seen since leaving the force—and the only one so close to her own home. Standing in the empty alley with the body left her with a vague sense of unease. The wind picked up, swirling through the garage entrance, and Annie felt the cold through her heavy woolen peacoat. Stuffing her free hand deeper into her pocket, she wished she'd worn her heavier knit cap. The long scar above her right ear was starting to ache. She rubbed it and wished Gunnar would hurry.

A town police car slowly pulled into the alley. The emergency lights on top of the cruiser were on, but the siren wasn't, which Annie considered a small mercy, given her current sensitivity to loud sounds. The officer parked diagonally, blocking the alley, then got out of the car. Annie stepped out of the garage to see who'd caught the call and recognized Officer Mike Hartt.

He smiled. "Detective."

"It's just Annie now, Mike," she said, smiling back but feeling a little twinge at the change in her status.

"Oh right. Sorry. I'm never going to get used to that." Mike had been on the force for only a few years when Annie left, but he'd been one of her students at the academy.

"It's fine," Annie said. She'd had a little trouble getting used to it herself.

"Dispatch said you found a body."

Annie pointed toward the wall. "See the leg?"

"Yeah. What do you think? Accident?"

Annie shrugged. "I'm guessing he fell. It was really icy last night. Can't be sure, though. He's covered in snow, and I didn't want to disturb anything."

She wouldn't have wanted to work the scene. Snow was a mess—not as bad as rain, but trace evidence was still hard to locate.

Mike got out his notepad. "When did you find him?"

"Just a few minutes ago. You'll see my tracks and my dog's. I didn't see any others."

He walked over to look at the body, careful to step in Annie's tracks. He cordoned off the area with yellow police tape and took photos of the scene.

Gunnar's unmarked car pulled into the alley a few minutes later. Annie watched as her former partner got out of his car like a Viking in a suit. He spoke to Mike. At six feet eight, Detective Gunnar Jansson dwarfed the other officer. Annie smiled. She'd missed the big man. He pulled on latex gloves and checked the man's pockets for identification. While she waited for him to come talk to her, two more patrol cars arrived in the alley.

Annie tried to figure out which shop owned the patio where the body was. It didn't belong to any of the restaurants. She counted from the corner vintner and ruled out the jewelry store and the spa. The property had to be Susan's Sundries, which had opened in the fall.

"Hey," Gunnar said, walking up to her. "How are you doing?"

"Aside from finding him"—she nodded toward the dead man—"I'm okay. Freezing but okay. I have an appointment in a little while, though. I need to get going." She pressed at the scar, which continued aching in the cold wind.

Gunnar nodded. "Sure, sure. I appreciate you waiting. You want to tell me what happened?"

Other police vehicles arrived behind him.

"There's not much to tell," Annie said. "I was walking my dog, and he noticed the body and started barking."

Gunnar held his hand out to Chester.

"He's missing an eye," Gunnar said.

Annie nodded. "I always said you were a great detective."

Gunnar snorted.

"He was like that when I found him," she said.

Being on this side of an interview with Gunnar was strange. The Leesburg Police Department didn't officially partner up their detectives, but people sort of gravitated toward each other, and Annie had usually worked with Gunnar.

"I don't suppose you walked him last night and noticed anything suspicious going on in the alley?" Gunnar asked.

"No. I don't walk him this way at night. This is our morning route."

"My old lab would be jealous," Gunnar said. "She's lucky if she gets walked a couple times a week."

Annie remembered how fat Gunnar's lab was. "It's good for both of us."

Gunnar smiled. "I can see that. You look great, Annie."

"Thanks."

She wished she could say the same of him, but Gunnar looked as though he'd put on a few pounds, and his face was redder than it should have been, even in the cold. His thick blond hair was shaggier than she'd ever seen it, and he needed a shave. When they'd worked together, he was always pressed and ready to go, so seeing him looking unkempt at all was weird even at this early hour.

While they were talking, Bernie Smith, the crime-scene tech, arrived. She knelt over the body and had Mike assist her in rolling the poor guy over. Annie couldn't see his face from where she was standing. The man was on his back with his hands frozen palms up. She thought he looked like Han Solo frozen in carbonite in *The Empire Strikes Back*.

A few minutes later, Bernie walked toward them. She pushed an errant hair off her forehead, which was too tan for this time of year. Looking around, she noted with disgust, "I hate snow." She exchanged hellos with Annie.

"What have we got, Bernie?" Gunnar asked, ignoring the snow comment. Like most Vikings, he enjoyed the cold.

"Not much. Did you check for a wallet?"

"Yeah, I didn't find any."

Bernie frowned. "Me either. No cell phone or keys?"

Gunnar shook his head. "What's a grown man doing walking around downtown without a wallet or car keys?"

"Was he mugged?" Annie asked.

"Too soon to tell," Bernie answered.

"Any idea what killed him?" Gunnar asked Bernie.

"Nothing definitive. There's a blow to the back of the head, but it's hard to tell out here if he got it falling or if someone hit him."

Annie had a sinking feeling in her gut, but she shook it off—not her problem.

"If he fell, then he was awake enough to roll over and get his hands under him."

"And then what? He passed out?" Gunnar asked.

"Maybe. The medical examiner might be able to tell. In the meantime, I think we have to treat this as a crime rather than an accident."

"Great," Gunnar said grimly.

"What time did it start snowing?" Bernie asked. "That'll help with time of death."

"I took Chester out at eleven thirty, and it was sleeting," Annie said.

A couple guys from a local funeral parlor unrolled a black cadaver bag. They would be transporting the body to the medical examiner's office in Manassas.

"I'll let you know what I find," Bernie said. She left them to coordinate the removal of the body.

Annie turned to Gunnar. "Is there anything else you need from me?"

"Not right now," he said gently as he touched her forearm. "It's good to see you up and around though, like your old self." The sympathy in his voice cut through her. He didn't mean it as pity, but it felt like that anyway.

Annie smiled. She'd really missed him. She'd really missed all of this. "It's good to see you too. Good luck with your case."

Gunnar nodded. "Thanks."

Then they just looked at each other for a long moment before Annie headed back to her apartment. Walking away from him was hard when an active investigation was going on, but she had to. This wasn't her life anymore.

CHAPTER TWO
Friday Morning

The snow was starting to let up, but the wind was blowing even harder as Annie stepped out of the shelter of the alley. She pulled her cap down over her ears and hurried home with Chester trotting alongside. Despite her best efforts, the walk was slow going. Standing around in the cold had stiffened her right leg, which made walking in the snow harder. When she took out her keys to open the door, she realized it was already unlocked. She hesitated, but Chester didn't. He nosed his way in, barking. Annie followed to find Ford sitting on her couch, trying to keep Chester from knocking over his coffee. The terrier was wiggling in his lap, trying to lick his face.

"Okay, okay," Annie said, making Chester get down. She smiled at Ford and hung her coat on the tall rack by the door. "You're back."

"Yep," he said, standing. He wrapped his arms around her, and she pressed her face against his broad chest, breathing him in.

"Three weeks is too long." Having his arms around her again was good.

He kissed the top of her head. "Sorry. I didn't really get a choice in the matter."

"I know. What time did you get in?"

"Late. Or, I should say, really early. About two o'clock this morning. I didn't want to wake you, so I stayed at my place."

Annie looked up at him. "I appreciate the courtesy." She slipped out of his arms and went to get herself a cup of coffee in her apartment's tiny kitchen. "How was Afghanistan?"

Ford snorted. "You're hilarious." He stretched. His dark hair was getting long. He usually didn't like it covering his ears or touching his shirt collar, but it was doing both, and he hadn't shaved for a while, possibly the whole time he was gone. His beard was full and thick.

She looked at him and smiled innocently. "What?"

"Do you really think I'll slip and tell you where I've been?" He folded his arms over his chest and arched an eyebrow at her.

"It could happen," she said, picking up the coffee pot.

"No, it couldn't."

"So says you. Can I top off your coffee?"

"Please." He held out his cup. "Are you doing okay? How are you feeling?"

"I'm good," Annie said, filling his cup.

"Really? Because you're rubbing your scar and limping."

Annie realized she was rubbing at the scar on her head and let her hand drop down to her side. "It's cold outside. I got a little achy and stiff. No big deal."

"If you say so," he said, his brow furrowed with concern.

She knew she should appreciate the concern. She knew it came from a good place, but it irritated her. "So, they don't have barbers where you were?" Annie said, changing the subject. "They don't sell razors?"

He smiled and rubbed his chin. "I'm trying a new look. You don't like it?"

"I like it fine. It's just different." She didn't like it, but Annie wasn't going to give him the satisfaction of saying so.

She hated his job. Like so many people in Northern Virginia, Ford was an information worker who couldn't discuss the nature of his business. She never knew where he was or what he was doing. He was very hush-hush-Secret-Squirrel, which irritated her, especially since his new look probably had more to do with work than it did with any interest in men's fashion.

"You know what?" he said, leaning over the bar and taking her hand. "Don't pour your coffee. Let's go over to the diner and get breakfast. My treat. I'm starving."

She didn't really feel like going back out in the cold, but if she said so, that would revive the conversation about her injuries. The restaurant was a short walk, which would give her a chance to get another peek at the investigation.

"Yeah, okay." She pulled her coat back on, but this time, she wrapped her neck with a heavy scarf her friend Celia had made, and she put on her woolen hat that had earflaps and a fleece lining.

"You be a good boy," she told Chester before they stepped outside.

THEY walked down Loudoun Street past the alley on the way to the restaurant. The police were still working the scene. Rotating red and blue lights were reflecting off the snow, making it look as though a lot more cop cars were there than actually were. Still, most of the department was probably in the alley and the town garage. Even the mere possibility of a murder in Leesburg would mean all hands on deck. Gunnar would be having everyone go over the scene with a fine-tooth comb—not an easy task in the snow and ice—on the off chance that the guy hadn't just fallen.

"I wonder what's going on over there," Ford said, stopping to look.

"Chester and I found a body this morning," Annie said, trying to keep the excitement out of her voice.

"What?" Ford said, whipping around to gape at her. "Why didn't you tell me?"

"It didn't come up. I was just happy to see you."

"Jesus Christ, Annie!" Ford looked exasperated. "What the hell?"

Annie held up her palms. "I know, I know. I'm sorry. I should have said something."

"You think?" Ford said. "What's the matter with you?"

Annie sighed. "Well, it's possible that I thought you might respond exactly like this. Calm down."

That gave him pause.

"I'm okay now. You don't have to freak out over every little thing."

"There is a dead man in an alley two blocks from your house. I'm allowed to freak out some over that."

Annie considered and decided he had a point. "Okay, you can freak out a little. But don't blow it out of proportion."

That seemed to mollify Ford, and he held up his palms in surrender. "I'm sorry. I just worry about you. I don't want you getting involved in this kind of stuff anymore."

Annie scowled at him. "I'm not involved. I made a phone call. It's not like I'm still a cop. I'm not working the case."

"Okay," Ford said, clearly sullen that she'd snapped at him. "No one you recognized?"

"I couldn't see his face. He was facedown and covered in snow and ice."

"How'd he die?"

"I don't know. Like I said, he was covered in snow. Anyway, that's not my job anymore." She couldn't help wondering, but she didn't share her interest with Ford, who was upset enough. Her stomach growled.

"Who's working the case?"

"Gunnar. Mike was there too." She looked over at all the police cars. "And apparently the rest of the department."

Ford's reaction was subtle, almost imperceptible, but he grimaced, his jaw clenching for just an instant. "So, how's Gunnar?"

"Good, I guess. It's not like we had a lot of time to chat." Ford had never liked Gunnar.

He hunched his shoulders against the wind and frowned.

Annie ignored it and continued past the alley. They turned the corner onto King Street and walked most of the way down the block toward the newly renovated Leesburg Restaurant. The new renovations were attractive and retro with a lot of chrome, and the seats were a lot more comfortable, but this was not the restaurant of her childhood. Annie missed the old place with its dark wood and uncomfortable church-pew booths. Worse, they no longer served egg-salad sandwiches, which Annie felt was a crime against humanity. But Ford still liked the place, so here they were.

The bell on the door rang cheerfully as they stepped into the restaurant. The smell of bacon frying and sausages sizzling wafted through the air—a welcome change from the cereal in her pantry at home. The room wasn't crowded, but Ford had a thing about sitting at the counter. He liked the middle because he could see the door and most of the restaurant from there. Annie preferred the privacy of a booth but didn't feel like arguing. Carrie, the waitress, poured them each a cup of coffee. Her blond hair was twisted into a sloppy bun secured with a couple pencils, and she pulled a pen from behind an ear.

"Did y'all see the police outside?"

"Yeah," Ford said. "Hard to miss them."

Carrie leaned in to whisper. "They say they found a dead man back there."

Annie nodded. Despite having grown dramatically in the past few decades, Leesburg was still a small town at heart. The guy in the alley would be all anyone talked about for a week, and if he'd been murdered, he would be the talk of the town for the foreseeable future.

"I wonder what happened. Do you think he just slipped on the ice, or do you think somebody killed him?"

Annie shrugged. "He probably just slipped."

Carrie nodded knowingly, as though mysterious deaths were what she thought about all day. "It's just like on that CSI show."

Annie didn't think so but didn't bother to point out why. She and Carrie had known each other for years, so she knew the only thing Carrie loved more than gossip was drama. Annie thought not engaging was best since she didn't want to talk about nothing but death all through breakfast.

"What can I get y'all today?" Carrie asked.

They both ordered coffee, fried eggs, and toast with a side of grits.

Carrie put the order in and brought them silverware. "You used to be a cop," she said to Annie. "You should call one of your buddies and see what they found out."

"I'm sure they're too busy to talk to me right now," Annie said, pouring some half-and-half into her coffee.

"Well, I don't care what he died of—it's going to be a while before I go back in that alley. I told Juan he could take out the trash."

Annie was pretty sure Juan always took out the trash, but she didn't say anything.

"Hey, did you see the 'Skins game last night?" Ford asked Carrie.

"Oh, yeah. You know I never miss a game. I tell you, if they'd played the rest of the season like they did last night, they'd be in the playoffs." She shook her head. "There's always next year."

"Hope springs eternal," Ford said, and they both laughed.

Carrie went to ring up another customer at the register. She asked if he'd heard about the dead man in the alley.

"You saw the game?" Annie asked Ford.

"Of course not. I was on a plane, and I hate watching sports on my phone, but I knew they were playing and thought you might appreciate a change of subject."

Annie chuckled. "Thanks."

Ford winked at her. "Anytime."

Carrie brought their food, and they ate their breakfast in companionable silence, their thighs resting against each other below the counter.

Ford leaned over and whispered in her ear, "Hey, want to go back to your place and catch up?"

Annie smiled at the euphemism. "I can't this morning. I have a meeting with a client."

"Oh?" he said, obviously disappointed.

"Cheating spouse."

Ford's brow wrinkled with concern.

"Relax. It's all perfectly safe."

"Right," he said without conviction.

She checked the time on her phone. "Actually, I should get going." She slipped off the stool.

Ford caught her hand, and she smiled at him. She had to give him points for tenacity.

"Maybe later." She gave him a quick peck on the lips and headed back out into the cold. The temperature had risen a few degrees, turning the snow back into freezing rain. The walk back to her apartment was slippery, made harder by the increasing stiffness in her right leg.

CHAPTER THREE
Friday Afternoon

An hour later, dressed in a navy worsted-wool business suit with a white silk blouse, she pointed her black Toyota Prius toward the Beacon Hill golf community just outside town. The car had been a gift from her father. It was the perfect vehicle for a private investigator because she could sit in it for hours with the air conditioner or heater running and not waste much gas. Sitting for hours in her car waiting to take a picture of someone was something she did a lot these days, so the car was a real blessing. Her father had wanted her to have a more reliable car than her old Jeep Wrangler. Annie hadn't thought a new car was necessary, but once she was able to drive again, her father insisted. Something about her almost dying had made him very generous. She hadn't refused the gift but kept her Jeep anyway. After all, it was paid for and had its uses.

Despite VDOT's attempts to stay on top of the weather, slick spots were still everywhere, especially on the neighborhood roads, and visibility was poor. Even though Annie was driving west against traffic, the drive took almost twenty minutes when it normally took less than ten. She regretted not having driven the Jeep as she pulled onto Hidden Gap Road and slid a couple of times on her way up the hill past the massive homes on Silver Charm Place. Annie smiled as she turned left onto Spectacular Bid Place, with its ever-so-slightly less-stately manors. All the roads in Beacon Hill were named after racehorses. The neighborhood dripped with pretension and new money.

She pulled into a driveway that curved through a broad, snow-covered lawn. She rang the bell but didn't have to wait. Laura opened the door as though she'd been standing by it all morning.

"Hello, Annie. Come in."

Laura Carlton was lovely in a completely put-together way that Annie had never quite been able to manage for herself. Laura's hair and nails were always perfect, and her clothes were expensive and conservative. Unfortunately, no amount of poise could protect her from Annie's news. Laura had suspected her husband was cheating on her, and Annie was there to confirm those suspicions.

Annie stomped her feet on the front mat to knock the slush off her shoes, and Laura took her coat as she stepped inside. The two-story foyer had a chandelier so large it wouldn't have looked out of place at the Kennedy Center.

"I just put the kettle on for tea. Would you like some?" Laura asked.

"That would be great," Annie said.

She followed Laura through a wide hallway of gleaming dark wooden floors into the kitchen, which was awash in stainless steel. The house was so large and open it felt like a museum. The taupe walls and brown-on-beige color scheme didn't warm the place up any either. Annie had been in hotels that were more welcoming.

Laura's lawyer, David Cohen, was seated at the table when they came into the kitchen. He stood to shake Annie's hand. He wore cufflinks in his white silk shirt and a tie bar under a silk tie that highlighted his blue eyes. Annie had seen him around town. As usual, Cohen's suit looked as though it cost more than Annie made in a month. Even the perfect cut of his salt-and-pepper hair was probably out of her price range. She'd been lucky to get work as an in-house investigator for Cohen, Strauss, and Associates Law Offices. They were right in downtown Leesburg and had a long history there as a quality law firm. Their regular investigator was out on maternity leave, and Annie had been filling in. She really wanted it to turn into a permanent job, but she was trying not to get her hopes up.

"How are you doing, Annie?" he asked.

"I'm good. Happy to be inside. It's pretty chilly out there this morning."

David smiled warmly. "Yes, thank you for coming out in this mess."

"Have a seat," Laura said, indicating the ornately inlaid kitchen table, which Annie was sure had cost more than all her furniture combined. Annie sat down and looked at the large, immaculate eat-in kitchen with soapstone countertops, a subzero refrigerator, and what looked like a professional Vulcan stove. By comparison, Annie could stand in the middle of her tiny kitchen and reach everything. Her refrigerator was a Magic Chef of indeterminate age, and her stove, in glorious harvest gold, was at least as old. She'd had to use fingernail polish on the dials to mark the settings, which had worn off long before she'd moved in.

Laura puttered around as though she wasn't entirely certain where everything was. Despite the fabulous equipment, the kitchen didn't look as though anyone ever cooked in it. Maybe it had been designed with caterers in mind. Laura seemed reluctant to talk, but David chatted about the upcoming forecast. After a few minutes, Laura set a lovely porcelain Lomonosov tea service on the table. Annie recognized the ornate blue-and-white pattern as one that her aunt liked.

"So, what do you have for us?" Laura asked, sitting opposite Annie.

Annie slid a large manila envelope of pictures across the table to David. "I should warn you there are five women in there."

A muscle in Laura's jaw twitched. "Five different women? Or five encounters?

Annie thought that was an odd question, but she said, "Five different women in five encounters."

Laura frowned. "He didn't even bother coming home last night."

"I'm sorry." Annie was surprised that Nick Carlton hadn't come home. He'd struck her as dedicated to being a lunchtime Lothario.

Laura sat straighter in her chair as if good posture could make the situation better. She ignored David rifling through the photos and poured the tea.

Annie took a sip. "I know you asked me to follow him for two weeks, but before I continue with the surveillance, I wanted to check with you. It's your money, but you have plenty now to take him to court and get a very nice settlement. Actually, showing him those pictures should be sufficient to keep you out of court altogether."

David nodded in agreement.

"How many do you think there are?" Laura's voice was tight as she reached for the envelope.

David stilled her hand. "We talked about this," he said. "You shouldn't look."

Annie hesitated. She didn't want to twist the knife, but she was pretty sure others existed. Still, she waffled. "I'm not sure. It's five so far. That's a lot of women to juggle. This is probably it."

Laura looked from one of them to the other.

Generally, in divorce cases, Annie dealt only with the lawyer because dealing directly with the spouse could get dangerous. She'd only agreed to meet Laura at her home because her lawyer would be present. Still, she'd been worried Laura would see the pictures anyway, so she'd used Photoshop to put large black bars across the faces of the women and obscured anything that might indicate where the photos had been taken.

Laura looked down at her tea as if answers were hidden there. "I want to be sure we have them all. Stay on it another week."

David looked as surprised as Annie felt.

"Laura," David said soothingly. "We have more than—"

"I want another week," Laura said firmly.

Annie wanted to jump for joy but managed to contain herself. She would have no trouble paying the bills this month. She could even put money into savings. She reined in her emotions and said calmly, "If you're sure that's what you want."

Laura sighed. "I'm sure. One more week."

"Okay, then."

Annie turned to David. "I'll call you next Friday, then."

He nodded grimly.

Laura was clearly exhausted by their conversation.

"Thank you. I'll see myself out," Annie said.

Laura didn't look at her.

WHEN Annie opened the front door to leave, Gunnar was coming up the walkway with a Loudoun County deputy she didn't know. Annie closed the door behind her and met them halfway.

"Hey, Gunnar. What's going on?"

"What are you doing here?" Gunnar asked, his brow furrowing.

"This was my appointment."

"This is the residence of the guy in the alley," Gunnar said. "We're here to inform the wife." He introduced the deputy as Darla Watkins.

Annie barely registered her name. The hair stood up on the back of her neck, and a chill ran down her spine. It didn't seem possible. She'd just taken pictures of Nick Carlton kissing a redhead yesterday afternoon. Regardless of how she felt about his morals, Nick Carlton had been full of life. Gunnar was going to have his hands full with suspects. Nick had been sleeping with at least five women, and who knew how many of them had other relationships with potentially angry boyfriends and husbands? Annie glanced back at the house, where Carlton's very distraught wife was sitting with her lawyer.

"So, you found his wallet?" Annie asked.

Gunnar shook his head. "No. Fingerprints. He was in a bar fight in college."

Annie ran her fingers through her hair and felt them brush against the scar. The news was a lot to take in.

"She a client of yours?" he asked.

Annie raised her eyebrows but didn't say anything.

Gunnar looked past her at the house. "Could be good for us."

"I don't think she's your girl. She just hired me to follow him for another week," Annie said.

"Might be covering," Gunnar suggested.

"Maybe, but I don't think so."

Gunnar cleared his throat. "Well, we'll take it from here. See that you don't get in our way. I wouldn't want you obstructing justice." He winked at her.

Annie smiled. "I'm not in the justice business anymore, kids. Knock yourselves out." She walked back to her car and got in, happy to be out of the cold but irritated at the sudden loss of income. She was surprised to find herself somewhat sad about Nick Carlton. She didn't actually know the guy, but she had spent a considerable part of the last week following him around, so she felt as though she knew him. She had even kind of liked him in spite of the fact that he was a lying, cheating bastard. He always had an easygoing smile on his face and seemed pretty affable. Still, his escapades had been bound to catch up to him eventually. *Too bad it had gone down the way it did.*

She sighed. So much for Nick Carlton, and so much for putting money into savings this month. She watched the officers go in, considered sticking around, but then changed her mind. The police had a job to do, and she'd essentially just lost hers. She was pretty sure Nick wouldn't be kissing anyone in the morgue.

As she drove home, she kept thinking about him lying dead in the alley and how he might have found himself there. She regretted telling

Gunnar she didn't think the wife had done it because, considering Laura Carlton's situation, she actually made a pretty good suspect.

ANNIE'S cell phone rang as she opened the door to her apartment. She answered and switched to speaker so she could talk while she changed clothes.

"Ms. Fitch, this is Mia at Sterling Rehab, reminding you that you have an appointment on Monday."

"Yeah, okay. I'll be there."

"Great. We'll see you then."

Annie flexed her right hand. She needed to do her physical-therapy exercises. She was good about keeping up with the walking, mostly because Chester had to go out. But while walking made her feel stronger, the exercises for her hand left her frustrated. She had regained full range of movement in all her fingers but still had very little grip strength. Even something as simple as writing with a pen was difficult after a minute or two. She was supposed to practice gripping a soft foam ball several times a day, but she wasn't as diligent about doing that as she had been initially. Sighing, she put the ball in her pocket, and she and Chester went outside.

The weather was still nasty, so they walked over to the field at the edge of the parking lot so that Chester could do his business. Annie dutifully squeezed the foam ball while she waited for Chester to pick a spot.

Her cell phone rang again. Celia was calling.

"Can I come out to your place this afternoon so we can drive in together?" she asked.

Annie couldn't recall what she was talking about. "What?"

"Joey's birthday."

"Oh shit." Annie had completely forgotten about her brother's birthday.

"You forgot, didn't you?"

"No. Yes. Crap. I've got to go. I need to go shopping."

"Okay, so I'll see you at five."

"Sounds good."

A few minutes later, Annie was driving past the alley on the way to pick up a gift for her brother. Several police officers were still working the scene, and she tried to ignore the sudden longing to be among them.

CHAPTER FOUR
Friday Evening

That afternoon, Annie and Celia listened to WTOP on the radio as they drove east on the Greenway toward Arlington. Any glimmer of hope for good traffic on a Friday was quashed by the weather, which persisted in vacillating between rain and sleet. Annie sighed. She hated driving east—or any direction, really—in rush hour. Even though they were technically going against traffic, a lot of cars were still on the road, and the weather wasn't helping. To add insult to injury, they were on the Greenway with its exorbitant toll. The Greenway would dump them onto the Dulles Toll Road, which would cost her even more money.

"So how old is Joey now?" Celia asked.

Annie thought for a second. "I'm thirty-one, so he's thirty-three." She was struck by the fact that so much time had passed. Playing Red Rover with Ford and his cousins in her grandparents' backyard seemed like just yesterday.

"Wow, I can't believe he's that old."

"We're lucky he's that old. Down Syndrome can really shorten your life expectancy. It's a lot better than it used to be, but still..."

"I know," Celia said sympathetically.

Annie tried not to be irritated about having to drive in rush hour to go to a party she had no interest in attending. She understood why her father did it, but sometimes she wished they could celebrate as a family, just the three of them, on a weekend, like reasonable people. She sighed and chastised herself for thinking that way. When they'd been kids, she'd resented all the attention Joey received. Every little thing he did was treated like a major accomplishment even though she had quickly outpaced him in milestones. Those memories made her feel selfish and guilty when she thought about them.

"Is Joey still working at the recycling center?"

"Oh yeah. He loves it there," Annie said, adjusting the windshield wipers to deal with the road spray kicked up by the cars in front of her.

"Isn't it a hassle for your dad to drive him out to Fairfax every day?" Celia asked.

"It's only three days a week, and it's not such a big deal now that Dad's retired. I think he kind of likes it—gives him a reason to get out. Besides, that's where we found Chester. So the whole family is big on the recycling center."

Celia smiled. "Fair enough."

"How was your day?" Annie asked.

Celia sighed. "Ridiculous horse drama. I swear this time of year, they stand around thinking up ways to make me crazy and cost me money. What have you been up to?"

Annie tried to decide how to answer that. She and Celia had been fast friends since having been randomly paired to share a dorm room in college. She knew that, like Annie's father, Celia was concerned about her working as a private investigator. Annie didn't want to worry Celia, but she didn't like keeping things from her either.

She sighed. "A guy I've been investigating died."

"What? And you're just telling me now? Way to bury the lead. What happened?"

Annie recounted the events of the morning.

"Wow. That's crazy. So what do you think happened?"

Annie paused. "This is going to sound weird, but it feels like murder. It hasn't been officially declared a homicide, though, as far as I know."

Celia grimaced. "When was the last time someone was murdered in Leesburg, especially in the historic district?"

Annie shrugged. "In any part of Leesburg, it's been a few years. As for the historic district, never that I know of. I'm sure it's happened. I should go on one of the ghost tours and find out."

"But you're not going to do anything, right?"

"I'm not, which feels really odd, but murder isn't my purview any-more," Annie said, moving the car into the E-ZPass lane. "It's not like I'm a detective anymore. I'm a private investigator. The Common-wealth of Virginia says the term 'detective' is reserved for the police. I handle stuff like divorces and insurance fraud now, not murders."

"Good," Celia said firmly. "Then you're done. Let the cops deal with it. That's for the best anyway. Like you need that on your plate."

Annie sighed. "Yeah."

But not being part of the investigation didn't feel right. She felt oddly connected to the Carltons—not exactly responsible but definite-ly involved—and she didn't like the implication that she couldn't han-dle a murder investigation. Just because she wasn't a cop anymore didn't mean she wasn't capable. She was on partial disability because of the limp and because she couldn't quite pull a trigger yet, but she still knew how to investigate.

WHEN they finally pulled into Annie's father's neighborhood, cars were parked on both sides of the street in front of his house. Because it was an older area with mostly brick, Foursquare-style houses built in the 1930s, the streets were tight. Annie had to thread her way through to park several houses down. They walked on a narrow sidewalk past lawns with mature oaks and maples. In the spring, all the yards would be bursting with color, but now everything was buttoned up for the winter. The large azaleas and forsythia looked ragged and wet.

"Big turnout this year," Celia said.

"Isn't it always?" Annie asked, picking her way carefully over the sidewalk, where roots had lifted many of the bricks. Arlington hadn't received as much snow last night as Leesburg had, so most of it had disappeared in the rain, which was too bad. Joey loved the snow. Having more of it would have been nice on his birthday.

Despite the fifty or so people milling about, Joey spotted them immediately when they walked in the door. "Annie!" As people made way, he ran over, all smiles, and hugged her tightly. "It's my birthday!"

"I know, Joey. I brought you a present."

He'd recently had a haircut. Annie hated it when her father had his hair cut so short. It made Joey's head look like an egg.

"Hey, Dad, Annie brought me a present."

Tall and slim, her father slipped through the crowd and kissed her on the forehead. He had the same buzz cut her brother had. Her father seemed to have found the only crappy barber in all of Arlington and appeared to go there exclusively. "Good to see you, kiddo. It's been a while."

"I know. I've been meaning to come out, but I've been working." She caught the grimace that appeared on his face for a fraction of a second.

"Work is good," he said, smiling.

Annie knew her father hated her job, though. He hated her being a private investigator even more than he had hated her being a cop, and he'd hated that plenty. Before he retired, he had been an aerospace engineer with Boeing. Her mother had been a nurse practitioner before she'd died in a car accident when Annie was seven. Her father thought being a private investigator was kind of seedy and that she could do better, safer work. She was sure nothing would make him happier than to see her ensconced in an office somewhere, but to her, that sounded like torture.

Across the room, Ford was standing with his parents. He raised his glass toward her and winked, which improved her mood considerably. He was right. She needed a drink.

"Celia, how are you?" Annie's dad said while Joey gave her a big hug.

Annie slipped away to the living room, where Ford was talking to his parents.

Annie loved Ford's parents. They were fabulous. His father could not have been more old-money Southern, and his mother could not have been more exotically eastern European. Ford's mother, Olga, whom everyone called Ollie, wore a deep-red woolen dress that set off her dark hair and eyes. Ollie was tall, slender, and beautiful, clearly where Ford got his good looks. His father, called Boo, was a couple of inches taller than Ford, with a booming voice and a big belly to match. He was in a three-piece, single-breasted navy suit with a white shirt and a golden tie. The suit was tailored perfectly and did what it could to disguise his belly. Officially, Boo was Buford Lee Otley, Jr., while Ford was Buford Lee Otley III. She smiled to think of Ford as Buford. He hated the name and had christened himself Ford by age seven. His grandfather was Big Boo to close friends and family. His father was Boo, so as a child, Ford had been called Booboo, which he hated even more than Buford. Annie had supported the switch to Ford, and eventually everyone else had come around except his grandmother, who still referred to him as Booboo.

"Annie!" Boo said and pulled her into a big hug. "How are you, darlin'?"

Ollie took Annie's hand. "How are you, dear?" she said in a voice still laced with a Russian accent despite decades of living in the US.

"I'm fine. I'm good."

"I'm so glad to hear it. You look good, not limping so much, and your speech is quite clear. You seem as good as new." Ollie said warmly.

"You do, baby doll," Boo added with a sympathetic smile that made Annie cringe inside.

"Thank you." Annie smiled and glanced at Ford, who looked mortified.

"We've, of course, been keeping up with your progress through Ford, but it's nice to see for ourselves how well you are doing."

"We don't see enough of you, Annie," Boo added.

"I know, but you know how it is when you first start a business," Annie said, happy to get off the subject of her health.

Boo nodded knowingly. "I know, girl, but you've got to take time for yourself too."

"You shouldn't push yourself so hard," Ollie added.

"We'll try to get out to the house soon," Ford said, draping an arm across Annie's shoulder. "How about we get you a beer?" He steered her away from his parents. "I am so sorry," he whispered in her ear. "Why do they always do that?"

Annie choked back a laugh, which came out as a soft snort. "Don't be. They mean well. It comes from the heart."

Ford clasped a hand over his eyes. "I know, but they don't need to be so specific."

"Don't worry about it." At least he understood, even if no one else in their families did, that she didn't want to talk about her recovery. For over a year, that had seemed like the only topic of conversation, so now that she was working again, she wanted to talk about something, anything else.

He reached into a cooler of ice her father had set up at the other end of the living room and pulled out a couple Port City beers. Her father was all about supporting the local brewery. Ford popped the cap off and handed it to her.

"Cheers." She tapped her bottle of Optimal Wit against his Essential Pale Ale.

He pulled her in for a hug, and she rested her forehead against his broad chest as he kissed the top of her head. For a moment, she forgot about all the people talking over each other.

She was about to ask Ford how his day had gone when her eighty-year-old great-aunt Ginny put her clawed hands on their arms. "When are you two going to get married?"

Annie opened her mouth, but Ford beat her to it.

"Just as soon as I can catch her," Ford said, patting Aunt Ginny's hand.

"Oh, dear, don't you think it's about time you let him?" Aunt Ginny asked, squeezing Annie's arm.

"He's just going to have to run a little faster," Annie said, rolling her eyes at Ford over her diminutive aunt's head.

He grinned back at her. She extricated herself from Ginny's grip and made her way through the crowd to the kitchen, which was slightly quieter than the living room. Her aunt Peggy was mixing punch at the sink.

"Do you need any help?" Annie asked.

"Oh, I've got this, sugar. Your Ford got here early and helped us set up all the chairs. He is so sweet and so handsome."

Annie looked at Ford in the living room, still chatting with Aunt Ginny. He was handsome at six feet tall with broad shoulders and a trim waist, olive skin, dark-brown hair, and clear-blue eyes so like his mother's.

"Yes, he is."

"I thought you two would have gotten married by now."

And this, thought Annie, *is why I hate family gatherings.*

AS the party progressed, a series of other friends and relatives all had something to say about her recovery. If they weren't asking about her health, they wanted to talk about Ford or her relationship with him. All the compassion and curiosity was exhausting.

Annie did appreciate the well-wishes, but the last time she'd seen many of these people, she'd either been in the hospital or in the middle of rehab. She'd looked bad after the shooting. She'd been shot three times, the last of which was a glancing blow to the head, leaving her with slurred speech, balance problems, and some loss of hearing in her right ear. The other two shots left her with the limp and the difficulty with her grip, but all those things were vastly improved. Her hair had finally grown back enough to cover the long scar on the right side of her head, so she could look in the mirror without being reminded of what had happened. Even so, she sometimes felt as though she'd recovered as a stranger, someone similar but not quite the same as who she used to be. Gatherings like this just served as another reminder of that.

Annie was thrilled when her father finally announced that the time had come for Joey to open his gifts, if only because all the attention would shift to him and people would stop talking so much. Following a conversation in a crowd was difficult for her. Everyone gathered in the living room. Elderly relatives occupied all the seats except one wing chair, where Joey sat like a king. He was even wearing a paper crown. Everyone else crowded into the room to watch. Joey opened every gift with such excitement and such gratitude that no one wanted to miss it. Annie smiled when he squealed as he opened the big paint set she'd bought him. Joey loved to paint. His easel was permanently set up in the sunroom at the back of the house. Annie watched as he pulled the next present toward himself, then her phone vibrated in the back pocket of her jeans. She glanced at the number. Gunnar was calling. She slipped out of the crowd and answered the call once she was in the hallway.

"Hey, Gunnar, what's up?"

"I was talking to Mrs. Carlton this afternoon. She showed me the pictures you took. You put a black bar across all their faces."

"Of course," Annie said. "That's PI 101. I can't show a distraught woman the actual faces of the women her husband is sleeping with. What if she knew one of them and went crazy and shot someone? Normally, I don't show them anything and only deal with the lawyer, but she paid extra for direct access to the evidence."

"Okay, sure. I get that. But did you ID any of the women?"

"No. I would only do that if her lawyer requested it for some reason." She continued walking down the hall toward the sunroom, which was quiet and out of everyone's earshot.

"Right. Then I need to see the unaltered pictures so we can ID them. The ME officially declared Nick Carlton's death a murder. Someone clubbed him in the back of the head with a rock. I need to see all of your photos, and I want to interview you. I need to know everywhere he went while you followed him."

"Sure, of course, no problem. When do you want to meet?"

The sunroom was covered in Joey's paintings. He loved cars, so cars were in almost every picture along with other things he loved, like their dad and Chester and Annie.

"How about right now?"

"Come on, Gunnar. I'm in Arlington at my brother's birthday party."

"I've got nothing on this, Annie. You know how it is. Every hour out from the crime, the chances of solving dwindle. It also doesn't help that the wife's lawyer was sitting in her kitchen when we made the notification. Help me out here." Gunnar was clearly desperate.

Annie chuckled. "Yeah, talk about lawyering up fast."

"It's not funny," Gunnar said.

Annie was still trying to wrap her head around the idea of someone being killed just a couple blocks from her apartment. "I can't believe there was a murder downtown."

"Yeah, I know," Gunnar said, "but the ME's preliminary report finds force consistent with a blow to the head, not a fall. There was also a small piece of rock and rock dust in the wound, but he was lying on brick."

Annie blew out a slow breath. She ran her fingers over a painting of her whole family standing in front of her father's old Mustang. It was one of her favorites and obviously one of Joey's too. He'd painted the same picture many times. Another one was on her fridge.

"Yeah, okay," she said. "Can you swing by my place in an hour? I keep the photos on my laptop, and I don't have it with me."

"Sure. See you then." Gunnar hung up.

ANNIE STARED OUT AT the backyard. Since the house had been built in the thirties, the plot was larger than the ones typically seen in new neighborhoods in Northern Virginia. She thought about the swing set they used to have back there and wondered what had happened to it. She remembered planting the dogwood tree on the first anniversary of her mother's death. Dogwoods were her mother's favorites. The tree was now twenty-five feet tall and flowered beautifully in the spring, but at the moment, it looked spindly and bare.

"Hey," Celia said from the doorway. "What are you doing out here? You're missing the best part."

"Yeah, but I've got to go. They declared Nick Carlton's death a homicide. Gunnar needs to interview me about the week I followed him."

Celia scowled at her. "Now? Didn't you tell him you were at your brother's birthday party?"

"Of course, but this stuff is time-sensitive, and you never know what's going to matter when you're trying to break a case."

"I don't see why it can't wait until tomorrow." Celia's disapproval was palpable.

"Because it can't. Do you want to come back with me, or should I ask Ford to drive you home later?"

Celia sighed. "I'll go with Ford."

"Okay. I really am sorry, but I have to do this."

Celia frowned, clearly annoyed. "If you say so."

"Thanks," Annie said and stepped out of the sunroom and joined the crowd around Joey. She caught Ford's eye and gestured with her head for him to meet her in the hall.

He joined her a moment later. "What's up?" he asked in a quiet voice.

She sighed and put her hand on his arm. "I've got to go. The police want to interview me about the guy I found in the alley."

"Gunnar wants to interview you?" he asked. "Seriously? Right now?"

"Yes, because he's in charge of the case and the clock is ticking," Annie said, trying to keep the irritation out her voice. "Will you tell Dad after Joey finishes with his presents? And can you drive Celia home?"

Ford frowned at her. "Sure." He obviously wanted to ask more questions, but he held his tongue.

Annie slipped out the front door without making a sound. She was ashamed of how relieved she felt about leaving the party. All the noise had given her a headache, and if one more person asked when she and Ford were getting married, she was going to scream. There was something wrong with her that made talking about evidence in a homicide so much more appealing than spending an evening with her family and friends.

CHAPTER FIVE
Friday Night

The rain had stopped, and the traffic had cleared considerably for the drive back to Leesburg, so the trip out didn't take nearly as long as the trip in had taken. That was typical of life in Northern Virginia, where everything revolved around traffic and no one spoke in terms of distance—only time. All long-term residents knew at least five ways to get everywhere they went regularly. Annie was proud of her own encyclopedic knowledge of the back roads in Loudoun, Fairfax, and Arlington counties.

Back in her apartment, she turned on her laptop, fed Chester, and took him out for a quick potty break before Gunnar showed up. When she opened the door, he was wearing the same rumpled suit he'd been in that morning.

"You look like you haven't had a break all day," Annie said.

"Probably because I haven't." He sighed. "This is a damn mess, Annie."

She felt bad for him. He must have been getting tremendous pressure to solve the case.

"Come on in," she said. "I'll show you what I've got." She closed the door behind him.

He handed her a file. "You show me yours, I'll show you mine."

"Okay," she said, smiling. "Take a seat. You want something to drink?"

"A glass of water would be great."

"Sure. The pictures are on the laptop. I've already opened the album."

Gunnar sank heavily onto Annie's leather sofa and pulled the computer into his lap. "Oh, God bless you," he said as she went to get the water.

"What?"

"You've labeled everything with dates, times, and locations."

Annie chuckled. "I'm all professional that way. Have you had anything to eat?" She set his water on the coffee table.

"I had a bag of chips at lunch."

She sighed. "You have to eat, Gunnar."

Annie looked at the folder he'd handed her. Not much was in it: crime-scene photos, Gunnar's notes from the scene, a preliminary autopsy report, a fingerprint set, Nick Carlton's DMV record, and the extremely brief arrest report from his college days.

"So the medical examiner thinks he died of hypothermia?" Annie asked, surprised. She'd expected the report to say he'd died from the head wound.

Gunnar looked up from the laptop. "Yeah, in the final analysis, the blow to the head wasn't enough to kill him, but it knocked him out. Lividity says he died how you found him, face down with his hands under him, like he was trying to push himself up."

Annie closed the folder and went back into the kitchen to make a ham sandwich. "Rough way to go. What did his wife say?"

"You mean what did her lawyer let her say?"

"Right."

Gunnar shook his head. "That guy. You work for him?"

"I'm on temporary contract with his firm. Cohen's all right. He's wound pretty tight, but he grew up around here. His mom's family owns a lot of land in the county. So, what did Laura say?"

"She said they had dinner at Lightfoot last night and had an argument, so she went back to the town garage and drove the car home without him."

"Wow. That's harsh." Annie wasn't surprised, though. Because Laura owned a successful real-estate firm in town and had a reputation for being tough and straightforward, Annie could totally see her leaving Nick to find his own way home.

Gunnar yawned. "Yeah. She said she thought he'd get a cab. When he didn't come home, she assumed he slept on the sofa in his office or with one of the women he's been seeing. A couple of the waiters at Lightfoot backed her up on the time of the argument. They said it got nasty and loud for a moment before she stormed out."

Annie wondered how long that moment was and which one of them got loud in public. Laura didn't seem like the type, but then neither did Nick. "I see. Do you like her for it?"

Gunnar scratched at the stubble on his chin. "She certainly has motive. He was cheating on her with anything in a skirt, and he was insured with a million-dollar policy."

Annie nodded and handed him the sandwich.

"Thanks," he said.

"I don't know. She didn't strike me as murderous as much as hurt, like she wanted all her ducks in a row before confronting him with his cheating. Besides, he'd probably pay out over a million in alimony in just a few years."

"That's if she was granted alimony. She has her own money, her own job, and no kids. We have Davis looking into their financials."

Gunnar took huge bites of the sandwich. He always forgot to eat when he was on a case, which would consume him until he brought it to conclusion. She'd always thought he was lucky he didn't work in an area with more crime.

Annie nodded. "Okay, but since she has her own money, that doesn't make the insurance much of a motive. The house they're living in is probably worth close to a million. She'd get half of that in a divorce."

Gunnar leaned back, locked his fingers behind his head, and considered the situation. "Clearly, it was a spur-of-the-moment thing. Nobody plans to club someone in the head with a rock. I'm trying to get footage from the ATM at the end of the street, but it was probably too dark to see anything. There's also a camera at the Exxon on Market Street. That'll show us if she actually left when she says she did instead of doubling back to the alley."

Annie considered that for a moment before responding. "Maybe, but she could have used the south exit from the garage."

"I know, and there's no camera that way."

"Besides, I can't see Laura lying in wait in the alley."

"It wouldn't have been like that," Gunnar said. "She could have been waiting in the alley for him to come back to the car, they argued again, and bang, she hits him in the head."

Annie shook her head. "Maybe. I don't know. I'm not seeing it. How was she when you talked to her?"

"That's the thing. She seemed genuinely shocked." He shrugged. "She's either a very good actress, or she didn't know he was dead." Gunnar turned back to the computer screen. "Maybe one of these women did it."

Annie sat next to him and looked at the screen. She pointed at a perky blonde with athletic good looks and a girl-next-door vibe. "Of the five, he only saw her more than once last week."

"Nice-looking woman."

"They're all nice looking," Annie said.

"No, I don't mean it that way. I mean she actually looks like a nice person whereas the other women look kind of... I don't know..."

"Wolfish?" Annie suggested.

"Yeah, kind of predatory and hard. Where did he meet all these women, anyway?"

"I wondered that myself."

"And?"

She shrugged. "And that's not really my job. I take pictures of the liaisons. I don't identify the women, and I never saw anything to indicate how he was meeting them, but my best guess is 'online.'"

Gunnar raised his eyebrows at her. "Online where?"

"Why, Gunnar," Annie said, teasing, "you're a married man."

He chuckled. "Like I've got time for an affair anyway. Seriously, where would you start?"

Gunnar understood that computers were valuable tools, but he believed real police work was done on foot, not on a keyboard. When they had worked together, he recognized that Annie's research skills were better than his and always deferred to her when it came to the internet or any kind of database work.

"I'm not starting anywhere. I'd have porn spam in my inbox for weeks. Besides, he could have had an app on his phone. Something like Tinder."

Gunnar sighed. "We're still looking for the phone. I'll check back with his business partner in the morning, see if he knows anything about it. Have you had any dealings with him?"

Annie shook her head. "I know his name is Eddie Peabody, but that's about it. I've seen him around but only because we both live in the historic district and there aren't that many people who do. Actually, he was recommended to me as an accountant and financial advisor by Ford's dad, but before I managed to make an appointment, Laura asked me to follow Nick, so I never called. All I know is that he and Nick have a business that operates out of an office in the back of Eddie's house over on Wirt Street: Carlton and Peabody Financial Services."

Gunnar nodded thoughtfully. "I thought accountants and financial advisors were different."

"I thought so, too, but Ford's father said Eddie is technically what they call an investment representative. He has his CPA, and he's done all the certification to buy stocks and stuff on behalf of his clients. Basically, Mr. Otley said there wasn't anything about money that Eddie doesn't know."

"Really? That's good information. Can you put these pictures on a thumb drive for me? I'll get them printed and get Stan started on identifying them."

"Sure, do you have one?" Annie asked, somewhat saddened by thinking of Stan as his partner now.

He fished around in his suit pocket and came up with a battered thumb drive. "I don't know how much room is on this one. Do you have another one I can borrow?"

Annie smiled and took it from him. "Sure."

"So, no idea who any of them are?" Gunnar asked hopefully.

"Being a PI isn't like being a cop, Gunnar. It's better not to have the information at all so if the client asks who they are, I can honestly say I don't know."

"Yeah, okay." He leaned back and closed his eyes while Annie downloaded the files.

She watched him while he rested, and she thought again that he looked really worn down, too much so for it to be just this case. She wondered whether all the stress was coming from work or home. She didn't know his wife well, but on the few occasions they'd met, she'd thought the match was weird. Gunnar was very down-to-earth and levelheaded while his wife seemed kind of fussy and high-maintenance. Gunnar opened his eyes and leaned forward.

"This sofa is really comfortable," he said. "I almost dozed off there for a second."

Annie smiled. "That's true. I have to sit at the table if I want to get serious work done." The sofa was undeniably the most expensive piece of furniture she owned. It was thick dark-brown American-made leather, with a distressed surface and down-filled cushions. She'd found it deeply discounted at an outlet because it had a nine-inch cut on the back. She couldn't have cared less about the cut because it faced the wall. The rest of her furniture was early garage sale or handed down from her father and aunts.

Gunnar stood and stretched his back. "I can see why."

"Any luck finding the murder weapon?" Annie asked.

He sighed. "No. It wasn't near the body, so chances are the killer took it."

"Great." Annie thought about all the old stone walls running through Leesburg. "So it could be anywhere."

"Exactly," Gunnar said.

While Annie switched out thumb drives to download all the pictures, they caught up on station gossip and were having a good laugh when Chester ran to the front door and started barking.

ANNIE got up to open the door but heard Ford's key in the lock. When he came in, she could tell he was irritated that Gunnar was still there.

"Gunnar," Ford said, his voice deeper than usual.

Gunnar stood and stuck out his hand. "Ford."

Ford's hand looked small in Gunnar's, which struck Annie as funny, but she suppressed a grin.

"Hey, how was the rest of the party?" Annie asked to break the tension.

"Fine, but your aunt Ginny spilled juice on me."

"Juice?"

Ford wiped at a dark stain down the front of his shirt. "Well, she said it was juice, but my shirt smells like vodka."

Annie smiled. "That sounds right. Come in back. I'll throw it in the wash."

But Ford took off his shirt right in the living room and handed it to Annie. She was sure he was flexing because every muscle was taut. She rolled her eyes and took it from him.

"How's it going, Gunnar?" Ford asked as she stepped into the bedroom to get him another shirt.

"Fine, Ford," Gunnar said. "How's it going with you?"

When she came back, Ford was standing with his hands on his hips, washboard stomach on full display. She hoped he wouldn't start peeing to mark his territory.

Before Ford could answer, Annie threw a T-shirt at his head. She pulled the thumb drive from her laptop and handed it to Gunnar. "That's the last of them."

"Thanks, Annie," Gunnar said. "I'll let you know how it goes."

"Great. Good luck."

"Thanks. See you later."

Annie saw Gunnar to the door before turning on Ford, who was now wearing the T-shirt and coming out of the kitchen with a couple of beers and big smile on his face.

"Why do you do that?" she asked.

"Do what?" he asked, clearly baiting her.

She didn't feel like giving him the satisfaction of an argument. "Nothing." She took one of the beers.

Ford glared at her. "Why was he here so late?"

"I was downloading photos for him. He wanted the RAW files, so it took a while." She really didn't want to get into this with him. One time, years ago, before he was married, Gunnar was drunk at a party and made a very clumsy pass at her. He was deeply embarrassed and humiliated the next day and apologized profusely. They'd worked together after that without so much as an inkling of impropriety. Unfortunately, Ford had been at the party and had never let go of what he perceived as Gunnar's interest in Annie.

"You want to watch a movie?"

"No," Annie said. "I think I'll go read." Sometimes she hated that, aside from the front door, the only door in her apartment was to the bathroom. The living room was separated from the kitchen by the four-foot-high bar, and the bedroom was separated from the kitchen by an eight-foot wall. A narrow hallway connected all three rooms, and the bathroom and laundry room were off the bedroom in the back. Generally, Annie liked the apartment. It had all the space she needed, and the twelve-foot ceilings, left over from when the building used to be a warehouse, made it feel bigger than it really was.

Unfortunately, whenever Ford irritated her and she needed a little distance from him, space was hard to find. She wished he would just go back to his house, a short walk down the street. Ford seemed to prefer her tiny apartment to his spacious old colonial, which she found ridiculous. She'd inherited her grandparents' house in Leesburg, but she rented it out for the income because the house rented for more than double what she paid in rent to Ford's father. Had she been able to afford it, she would have lived there rather than in the glorified hallway that was her apartment.

CHAPTER SIX
Saturday Morning

Annie awoke to Ford kissing her on the forehead.

"I'm heading out," he said.

"Okay." She looked at the clock radio on her nightstand—only five thirty. She lifted herself up on one elbow. "Why so early?"

"Sorry about that. I need to pick up some stuff at my place before I go into work."

"Will I see you tonight?"

"I'm not sure. I'll call you." He winked at her.

"All right." Annie fell back against the pillow.

She listened as Ford locked the front door behind him. Sometime later, Chester jumped up on the bed and licked the tip of her nose, waking her again.

"Stop. No licking," she said as she pushed him away, but she got out of bed anyway.

Chester seemed to fully understand that going out was Annie's responsibility. He never pestered Ford to take him out even if Ford was the first to get up in the morning.

"Okay, buddy, let me put some clothes on, and we'll go."

As she pulled on jeans and a sweatshirt, she hoped this morning's walk would be much less eventful than yesterday's. *At least it isn't as cold,* she thought as she stepped out into the early-morning air. The sun was just up, and yesterday's rain had washed most of the snow away, leaving everything shiny and wet but not frozen. She didn't want to tempt fate, so rather than walk over to Loudoun Street and past the town garage, she took their evening path toward the old churchyard. At first, Chester tugged in the direction of the garage, clearly not wanting his evening route in the morning. Terriers were creatures of habit.

Annie smiled at the little dog. "Come on, buddy. We're going this way today."

Chester looked at her with undisguised consternation, but he followed anyway. Annie liked this route. It took her through the residential area adjacent to the old downtown and past her grandparents' house, so she could keep an eye on the property and make sure the renters were taking care of things.

She liked to cut through the Methodist cemetery at the site of the Old Stone Church. The church had been torn down in 1900, but archeologists identified the original foundation in the 1960s. Annie liked to walk through the historic graveyard and then loop back toward her apartment.

She loved Leesburg, especially the historic district. She knew each of the clapboard houses and their shaded lawns so well that even the slightest change caught her eye. Some of the homes had been fully restored and were in great condition, others less so, but each place had its own charms. She'd spent every summer here while growing up, so summers until she turned eighteen had been all about being in Leesburg with her grandparents and Ford, whose family lived next door. They had roamed these streets every summer as children and later as teenagers. Joey and her father had stayed in Arlington but frequently visited on the weekends. Annie cherished the memories now, but that first summer, she'd felt as though she were being dumped in Leesburg because her father didn't want to deal with her.

She was happy to see that her grandparents' house looked good. The renters were a young couple who both worked in telecom. They paid their rent on time and kept the place tidy, which was a relief. She silently renewed a vow to eventually move in there, but knowing they were taking care of the place in the meantime was nice.

Chester nosed along the brick sidewalks, stopping to pee periodically, while Annie mused about the neighborhood. They turned into the old Methodist cemetery and walked past the remains of the church foundation and into the graveyard. She liked walking among the worn stones and reading the faded names. That gave her a sense of being part of a greater whole. She was careful not to let Chester pee on the graves, so she sighed when he stopped yet again. She was used to the stop-and-start nature of their walks and didn't think too much about it until Chester wouldn't move on. He was sniffing at a softball-sized gray rock in front of Captain Wright Brickell's headstone. The captain's was the older of the two oldest markers in the cemetery. The inscriptions on the headstones were no longer legible, but a plaque on the roof of a little shelter built over them noted the names and the date, 1777.

"Leave it," she told Chester.

Instead, he started clawing at it. Annie assumed he was trying to get at some unfortunate mouse or vole hiding between the rock and the headstone. Once Chester was onto a rodent, only picking him up would get him to stop. Annie leaned over to scoop him up and saw the rock he was digging at had something stuck to it. She felt a sinking sensation in the pit of her stomach. *Hair and blood.*

"Dammit." She picked up the little terrier. "You're killing me, Smalls." She pulled her cell phone from her pocket and called Gunnar.

"Jansson," he answered.

"I think I found your murder weapon," Annie said, trying to suppress her curiosity. This wasn't how she'd intended to start her day, but it was certainly more interesting than what she'd had planned. She knew it wasn't her case, but the thrill of finding a lead still ran through her like a shiver.

"Seriously?" Gunnar said. "Where are you?"

"At the Old Stone Church cemetery on Wirt Street."

"I'll be right there." His chair scraped back, and his keys jangled before he ended the call.

Annie looked around at the tiny, familiar churchyard with its aging headstones across from the foundation of the erstwhile Methodist church. She took a deep breath and let it out slowly. The adrenaline rush that usually accompanied the discovery of significant evidence washed over her. She reminded herself that this hunt was not hers, but the edgy excitement remained.

TEN minutes later, Gunnar pulled up his unmarked car next to the curb. Annie was standing under the gazebo marking the spot where the church used to be.

"We've got to stop meeting like this," Gunnar said, smiling.

Annie chuckled. "Tell me about it."

"What happened?"

"I was walking the dog. He wouldn't leave a rock over there alone." She pointed at the sheltered headstones.

They walked over to the old headstone, and Gunnar wrinkled his brow and leaned down to take a closer look at the rock. He examined it for what seemed like a long time as Annie waited impatiently for him to say something.

Finally, he stood, stretching his back out as he did so. "It does look like blood and hair. What the hell is it doing here?"

They both looked around the cemetery as though the killer might be hiding behind a headstone.

"I have no idea. Maybe it isn't what it looks like. Maybe someone used it to kill a rat or something." She smiled at him.

Gunnar snorted. "Yeah, maybe. I've got the crime scene tech on her way over here to check it out."

Annie nodded. "Sounds like a plan. I really need to get going, or I'd wait with you. I told Randall I'd get his mom's breakfast today."

Gunnar wrinkled his brow. "It's weird you found the body and what looks like the murder weapon."

Annie laughed and arched an eyebrow at him. "Am I a suspect?"

"Of course not." He shifted his feet and looked apologetic. "Not to me. I'm just saying there might be those that question, that's all. You know, I might have to bring the state in on this for added manpower. They're going to have questions of their own. You knew the deceased, you were following him, you found his body, and now you've found what looks like the murder weapon."

She frowned at him. "Yes, because he was killed in my neighborhood and apparently my dog is part bloodhound. You think that doesn't freak me out? You think I'm not shocked that the guy I've been following is dead now? Say what you will about his proclivities, but I didn't want Nick Carlton dead, Gunnar. I wanted him very much alive so I could follow him for another week and make a big, fat paycheck."

"Hey," he said calmly. "I know that. It's not like I think you're involved in this. I'm just telling you how it's going to look to someone who doesn't know you."

She sighed. "Right. Well, I guess I'll cross that bridge when I come to it."

"Of course," Gunnar said. He didn't look at her. "Do you have a lawyer?"

She raised her eyebrows in alarm. "You think I need a lawyer?"

He shrugged awkwardly. "Might not be a bad idea, just in case. I mean I know you're still in the police union as a retiree, but I'm not sure you'd qualify for a union lawyer for this. Might want to find that out."

She couldn't believe what she was hearing. She couldn't afford a lawyer. She glared at him for a long moment before saying, "I've got to go."

"Annie," he said. "Annie!" he shouted after her.

She ignored him and kept walking. She had errands to run. Instead of going home, she and Chester went to Shoe's Café. Her mind was spinning, and she didn't know what to think or how to feel about what Gunnar said or even about Nick Carlton's death.

When she reached Market Street, Annie heard someone shout her name and turned around. A woman in a long, royal-blue trench coat was rushing toward her, heels clicking against the brick sidewalk. She had short brown hair cut in a severe, angular bob. Her purse was big enough to hold Chester.

"Hi," she said breathlessly. "I've been trying to track you down for ages."

"Oh yeah? Who are you?" Annie asked, irritated at the interruption.

"I'm Dawn Sullivan with *Loudoun Daily News*. You're the one who found Nick Carlton's body in the alley."

Annie frowned. She knew all the local reporters, but she'd never heard of this woman.

As if she knew what Annie was thinking, Dawn smiled. "I only just got the job. My husband and I moved here from New York last month. He works for the county."

Annie sighed. "I'm not interested in talking to the press about an active investigation."

"So you're investigating his death too? Are you collaborating with the police? Or are you running an independent investigation?"

Annie mentally kicked herself. The active investigation line had fallen out of her mouth, a leftover from her time on the police force, when all questions from the press were directed to the public information officer. Unfortunately, Annie no longer had access to a PIO, although at the moment, she was wishing she did. "No comment" was all she said.

"Come on, Detective Fitch. This is big news in the community. You live right downtown. You must know how concerned your fellow citizens are and how much they need information. Don't you think the public has the right to know what's going on?"

Annie pursed her lips. "Fine. The police are allocating all their resources to relentlessly pursuing Nick Carlton's killer. I'm sure they'll
have a result soon."

The reporter's brow furrowed. "And what are you doing on this
case, Ms. Fitch?"

"Let's go," she said to Chester and walked away from the reporter as
quickly as she could without actually breaking into a run.

If Sullivan was new in town, she must have been getting her information from someone else at the paper. Unfortunately, since the shooting, Annie was well-known in the community. Crime was exceptionally
low in Loudoun County, so an officer shot in the line of duty had been
very big news.

LIKE a lot of restaurants in Leesburg, Shoe's had a dog bowl full of
water outside its front door. Annie let Chester get a drink before she
picked him up. Technically, dogs weren't allowed in the café, but Annie
found if she held Chester in her arms and got her order to go, no one
seemed to mind. She ordered two fried-egg sandwiches and took an apple and a banana from a basket on the counter. That way, Miss Mabel
could have the fruit for a snack later. While she waited, Annie looked
around the restaurant, which used to be a shoe-repair place. The marble
counter where the cash register sat had been in the building for more
than a hundred years, according to a little plaque next to it. She loved
the repurposing of the old building and looked forward to the opening of their "secret garden" in the back when the weather warmed up.
Eating back there and playing bocce was always fun in the spring. The
cashier interrupted Annie's longing for nice weather by handing over
her order in a brown paper bag.

"Here you go, Annie."

"Thanks, Jane," she said.

As if to mock her longing for springtime, clouds rolled in as she walked toward Miss Mabel's little brick townhouse. It was nestled between an office building and the apartments where Annie lived, a remnant of an earlier time in the town's history. The house had a long, narrow backyard and on-street parking. Miss Mabel had lived in the house since she was a little girl. Now she was seventy-eight, and with the help of her devoted neighbors and six children, she was able to remain in her home.

When Miss Mabel opened the door, the heat from inside hit Annie like a warm oven.

"Good morning," Annie said. "I brought you some breakfast."

"Oh, aren't you sweet? And you brought that good boy with you."

Annie let Chester off his leash, and they followed Miss Mabel into the kitchen. Annie pulled the sandwiches out of the bag and set them on the table.

"I made coffee," Miss Mabel said as she stroked Chester's back.

Annie got them each a cup and sat down at the table.

Chester sat on the floor between them and waited patiently. He knew better than to beg openly, but he also knew patience was always rewarded.

"Did you hear that terrible news about the Carlton boy?" Miss Mabel asked.

"Yes," Annie said, wondering how Miss Mabel always seemed to know everything going on in town even though she never left her house anymore. "Just awful." Her cell phone vibrated in her pocket, but she let it go to voice mail.

"My youngest, Raymond, used to play football with Nick Carlton."

"Is that so?" Annie asked, unwrapping the sandwiches.

"Oh, yes. They both played for County. Raymond went on to play for the University of Tennessee, and Nick played at Virginia Tech. Nick was such a handsome boy and so sweet. You know he brought me chocolate-covered cherries every year for Christmas?"

"I didn't know that," Annie said, trying to reconcile this new information with the Nick Carlton she'd been following. Apparently, he loved all women, young and old alike.

"Yes, he did. He found out I liked them when he was in high school, and he brought me some every year. Always had a big smile on his face. It's such a shame he's gone now, and so young." She shook her head.

Annie patted her hand.

"I know he's with Jesus," Miss Mabel continued.

Annie wasn't so sure about that, but she nodded anyway.

AS she and Chester walked home a little while later, Annie wondered if Ford had known Nick Carlton. Ford had gone to Loudoun County High School and was on the football team. Annie had gone to H-B Woodlawn in Arlington, which didn't have a football team, so she'd never even heard of Nick Carlton before his wife had called her. She recalled his easy smile and tried to shake the image, but it stuck. Watching someone closely for a week was an inherently intimate activity. She couldn't help but feel as though she knew Nick Carlton, and she wanted to know who had killed him, if for no other reason than his death seemed to be impacting her life. She was still smarting from Gunnar's comment about her involvement, largely because she knew he was right. Someone was bound to wonder why she kept stumbling upon leads. Annie was wondering that, too, which made her all the more curious about who had killed Nick.

CHAPTER SEVEN
Saturday Afternoon

After spending the rest of the morning and most of the afternoon following up on background checks, Annie fixed herself a cup of Irish breakfast tea. She took a few minutes to enjoy the warm drink and skim through the *Washington Post* online. The paper had a big story on the murder. The happenings in Leesburg didn't often make the *Post*, which meant more pressure on Gunnar. Loudoun had a large population of federal employees who, like Ford, commuted into DC. She was sure they would all be stirred up at the reality of a murder in what they considered their oasis away from the city. After finishing the article, she listened to her voice mail. She had missed several messages last night. They were all from reporters, including Dawn Sullivan. She erased them all. Her phone buzzed in her hand. Gunnar was calling.

Annie sighed and answered.

"Hey," Gunnar said. "Can we talk?"

Annie sighed again. "Sure."

"I'm outside your apartment."

Annie laughed and opened the door.

Gunnar stepped inside looking appropriately contrite. "I'm sorry about this morning. Obviously, I know you didn't murder Nick Carlton."

"Obviously," Annie said flatly.

"But just to make sure I've got all my ducks in a row, I need to officially interview you."

Annie raised an eyebrow at him. "Interview me about what?"

"Finding the murder weapon. Trailing Nick. Everything."

Annie frowned. "Are you serious? I already told you all that."

Gunnar shifted on his feet. "But not in an official capacity. I need to have notes to put in the file. Then no one can come along behind me and say I overlooked stuff because of our personal relationship."

Annie nodded. "Yeah, okay. I get that. Take a seat."

Gunnar looked relieved to be off his feet as he settled into the sofa. "This is really just about setting up the prosecution. You know that. I mean, we've got oodles of suspects way better than you. This guy wasn't just getting the occasional piece on the side. Your boy could be the poster child for sexual addiction."

Annie rolled her eyes. "That's right. Nick's my boy."

Gunnar smiled and then got serious. "This case is kind of a nightmare. The news people are all over it. We've got TV crews, print reporters, and even some damn bloggers wandering around downtown. The town council is all over the chief for a quick result, so the chief is all over me."

Chester jumped onto the sofa and sat next to Gunnar, leaning against him. Gunnar patted the little dog's head.

"You know what they say," Annie said. "Shit rolls downhill."

"And boy, is it ever rolling." Gunnar stared at his feet. "The problem is they can't lift prints off the rock, but the hair and blood are a definite match for Nick Carlton."

Annie shrugged. "It's freezing outside. Whoever did it was probably wearing gloves."

"Sure, and trace at the scene is worthless. People walk through that alley all day long."

Annie knew the alley was a popular shortcut. She used it all the time.

"We still can't find his wallet," Gunnar continued, "and his wife says he was wearing a watch. We haven't found that either. I thought we had something when we found his phone."

"You found his phone?"

"Yeah, it was tossed down that narrow little space between the jeweler and the spa."

"Terrific. Any prints?" Annie asked.

"Tons. We got everyone's prints. Apparently, Carlton was forever leaving his phone places, so people were always picking it up and giving it back to him. So we've got his prints, his wife's, his business partner's, his secretary's, a waitress at the Leesburg Brewing Company, who was apparently drunk and disorderly on several occasions when she was in college, which probably explains why she didn't graduate. And finally, we have three prints that weren't in the system, plus a lot of smudges and partials that weren't identifiable."

"Wow," Annie said. "That's a lot of prints."

Gunnar let his head drop back against the sofa. "Yeah." He rubbed his eyes.

"You look beat. Can I get you anything? Glass of water, maybe?" Annie asked.

"That would be great." He sighed. "At least his business partner knew which website he used to hook up with all those women. Get this: it's called Better than Lunch."

Annie chuckled as she went into the kitchen. "Clever. It sounds so benign."

"Right? The tagline is 'We know what you're really hungry for.'" He rolled his eyes.

"Gross." Annie got a glass of water from the tap.

"Yeah, so now we're trying to get a warrant to get the real names behind the user IDs of the women he was with from the website. Then when we finally do get the names, we're going to have to interview a lot of women. So you can see why I've got to make sure I don't miss anyone, including you."

"Sure. Otherwise, you hand the defense reasonable doubt because you didn't interview everyone with a motive." Annie smiled as she walked back over the sofa and handed him the water.

"Right."

He downed the water in one go and then asked her all the same questions he'd asked that morning, plus several others concerning the week she'd followed Nick. He carefully made notes of dates and times.

When he was done, Annie leaned back on the sofa. "You know, a missing watch and wallet makes this sound like a mugging gone wrong."

Gunnar sighed. "Sure, but who picks a big guy like Nick to mug? Not to mention, who mugs someone with a rock?"

Annie shrugged. "Neanderthal?"

He gave her a withering look. "Very funny. I think this had to be some kind of altercation that ended with a blow to the head."

"But it was a blow to the *back* of the head," Annie said. "Were there any defensive wounds on Nick's hands?"

Gunnar shook his head. "No, so I'm thinking words were exchanged. Nick turned to walk away, and bam, he's knocked in the back of the head."

"So the killer took the watch and the wallet to make it look like a mugging gone wrong?"

"Maybe. Or maybe the killer decided he might as well make a little money since he'd already killed the guy," Gunnar said grimly.

"Nice," Annie said.

Gunnar shrugged.

"So you're checking pawn shops for the watch?"

"Stan's calling places from here to DC, although I don't have high hopes for that."

"Why?"

"The wife said Nick wore an old Citizen watch he got in high school. It was engraved 'Best All Around' with the date 1997. Wouldn't be worth much now, and the engraving would be a dead giveaway, so I'm guessing once the killer saw that, he would have ditched it like the phone, which by the way, was also engraved."

"Really? What did it say?"

"Just his initials. Apparently, the Carltons are big on engraving."

Annie smiled. "They say the rich are different."

Gunnar chuckled. "Yeah." He yawned and stood, stretching. "I need to compare this to the notes I already have and get it all in the computer before I head home."

Annie walked him to the door. "Try to get some rest."

"I will," Gunnar said.

FORD was coming up the sidewalk as Gunnar was leaving. The two men raised their chins at each other.

"What was he doing here?" Ford asked as Gunnar got back into his car.

"He was questioning me about the murder."

Ford scowled at her. "Seriously? He thinks you did it?"

Annie laughed. "No. He's just being thorough. Chester found the murder weapon on our walk this morning."

Ford held up a hand. "Stop. What do you mean he found the murder weapon?"

Annie described what had happened at the Old Stone Church.

Ford let out a low whistle. "What the hell?"

Annie sighed. "Exactly. Gunnar doesn't want anyone thinking he's overlooked me because of our history. It's shaping up to be an ugly case."

"I imagine murder usually is."

Annie didn't disagree and thought it best to change the subject. "Where have you been?"

"I went to the gym. How do you feel about dinner and a show? My treat."

Annie smiled. "I feel good about it."

They walked the two blocks to the Tally Ho Theater and got tickets for the eight-thirty show. Annie liked the little historic theater that had been turned into a small venue for bands. Tonight, Suzy Bogguss was playing. Annie liked her eclectic mix of music and was happy that Ford wanted to go.

On the way to the Thai Pan for dinner, he wrapped an arm around her and held her close, which was very snuggly for Ford. He wasn't generally so affectionate, especially in public, so Annie couldn't help wondering what had gotten into him.

The Thai food distracted her, though. She'd been skeptical when the Thai place opened in one end of the gas station next to the county parking garage. Although the convenience store of the gas station was disconcertingly visible through a side door of the restaurant, the food was surprisingly good.

After Annie ordered pad thai and Ford ordered drunken noodles, she asked if he'd ever known Nick Carlton.

"I knew who he was when we were in high school, but I didn't really know him. He probably wasn't even aware that I existed. He was a senior when I was a freshman."

"But didn't you both play football?" Annie asked.

Ford laughed. "When he was varsity, I was JV. That's like being on different planets."

"Oh." Annie's high school didn't have a lot of sports, so the whole culture of it was somewhat lost on her.

"I knew his buddy, Eddie, though."

"Eddie, his business partner?"

"Yeah, Eddie Peabody, kind of nerdy. Nice guy, though. He was the statistician for the baseball team." Ford puffed his chest out. "You might not know this, but as a freshman, I was on the varsity baseball team."

Annie did know because Ford had told her more than once, starting the day he'd made the team. "I think you might have mentioned that before," she said, smiling.

Ford shrugged and sipped his Thai iced tea, a sweet concoction of spiced tea and evaporated milk. "Those two were really tight. The rumor in high school was that Eddie did all of Nick's homework."

"Really?" Annie said, raising her eyebrows. "Just how tight were they?"

Ford chuckled. "Not like that. Nick was a big horndog. I don't think he missed dating many of the girls in the high schools around here."

"Nice," Annie said. "Seems like that never changed."

"That doesn't surprise me," Ford said. "He had quite the reputation back then."

The waitress brought their food, and Annie let the topic drop.

Ford was in a good mood. He continued chatting about high school and then about the band they were going to see after dinner. He kept commenting on how good the food was as he picked up mounds of spicy noodles with his fork. Talking so much wasn't normal for him, and it bothered her. She couldn't help wondering if he was finally going to take another long-term assignment overseas. He hadn't left for a significant period of time since she'd been shot, but she knew he was being pressured at work to go for longer than the occasional few weeks he'd done recently. The last time he'd been this chatty and affectionate, the evening had ended with an announcement that he'd be gone for a year. Annie lost her appetite.

As they were leaving the restaurant, Annie suggested they go the long way around to the theater to avoid any reporters that might be lingering downtown. Ford was amenable and slipped his arm around her shoulders again as they made their meandering way back to the theater. Annie wished they could always be like this.

Suzy Bogguss played a great set, but Annie couldn't shake the feeling that something was going on with Ford, which dampened her enjoyment of the show.

ANNIE had trouble sleeping that night. She pulled herself up on one elbow and looked at Ford in the dim glow cast by the skylight. She smiled at how he'd turned out, nothing like the seven-year-old she'd once known. He was so skinny back then, all arms and legs. He always won when they raced from the mailbox in front of her grandparents' yard to touch the old pear tree in the back of his parents' house. He always won, but she never stopped agreeing to race. Then came the summer they both turned sixteen when she almost caught him. She grabbed the back of his shirt, which caused him to trip, and they both went tumbling under the pear tree. That was the first time he'd ever kissed her and the last time they'd raced. She sighed at the memory and rolled onto her back and stared up at the skylight. *My racing days are long behind me,* she thought as she rubbed at her right leg. The muscle in her thigh that had taken the bullet had a tendency to tighten and stiffen during the night.

She thought about Ford's jolly mood that evening and wondered again at what it meant. Supposedly, he worked for the State Department, but Annie suspected he worked for another agency entirely. She didn't have any proof, but a lot of people in the DC Metro area claimed to work for the State Department when they really worked for the CIA, the NSA, or certain departments within Homeland Security.

Ford had joined the military out of college when Annie had joined the police department. Annie had a double major in psychology and communications from George Washington University, while Ford had gone to Georgetown. He'd majored in international relations with a minor in Russian. They'd seen each other during college but not as often as the proximity of the two schools would imply. They were both serious students, but their time together was anything but serious. Back then, whenever they were together, they had a tendency to regress a bit into a sort of playful silliness. They were always casual in regard to their physical relationship. They each dated other people in high school and in college, but if they both happened to be single at the same time, they would pick up where they left off. The last year and a half was the longest unbroken period that they had been together.

After college, Ford had joined the army. When he returned from Afghanistan, Annie hoped that meant the two of them could settle into a more normal life, but within a week of returning home, he had a federal job with "the State Department." Within a few months, he was back overseas to parts unknown, at least to Annie. She looked at Ford, lying next to her, softly snoring, one arm thrown over his head. He slept so soundly that imagining he had a head full of state secrets was hard. Maybe he didn't. Maybe that was all in her imagination.

She rolled over and fluffed up her pillow, trying to get her head to shut up. Chester was sprawled in his little bed on the floor, sound asleep. Annie couldn't help feeling slightly jealous as she fell back against her pillow. Chester had had his own troubles in his short life. He was half starved and missing an eye when they'd found him, but now he was a normal weight of twelve pounds and slept like a log. If missing an eye bothered him in any way, he didn't show it. Annie wanted to sleep like that, sprawled out without a care in the world. But she did care, and that was the problem.

She thought about Nick Carlton's body lying in the snow. Finding his killer wasn't her business, but she was connected to the case now, and the last thing she wanted was an increase in questions about her involvement. She considered Laura Carlton as a suspect but quickly dismissed that idea. The murder seemed too impulsive. Lashing out with a rock just didn't seem like the kind of thing Laura Carlton would do. It was too spontaneous. She was too tidy, too controlled. Annie had trouble even imagining Laura picking a rock up off the ground. Annie could see Laura Carlton hiring someone to kill her husband, but hired killers didn't club their targets in the head with a rock in a public alley either.

She fell asleep thinking about who could have done it.

CHAPTER EIGHT
Sunday into Monday

The next morning after a late breakfast, Ford and Annie took Chester and walked over to Ford's house, which was on Church Street. It had been built in the early 1900s, and it belonged to Boo. Ford rented it from his father for next to nothing, but he had paid for some upgrades himself. He had the breaker box replaced to upgrade the electricity, and he had the whole house painted white inside and out. Annie tried to talk him into some more interesting colors, but he kept the house white with black shutters, as it had always been. Most Sundays were spent watching football on Ford's huge TV, and today was no exception.

Ford made popcorn on the stovetop with a popcorn maker his mother had given him for his birthday. Ollie was convinced that microwave popcorn was poisoning America. Ford said he just liked the way the stovetop popcorn tasted. He usually made it into kettle corn by adding a little sugar. Annie got each of them a beer, and they settled on the sofa for several hours of gridiron action. Between games, action of a more personal nature often took place.

Chester, used to the routine, snoozed in Ford's old leather recliner. Before the night game came on, they took Chester for a long walk through town. Ford had his arm draped over Annie's shoulders as they strolled through the neighborhoods looking at all the Christmas decorations. They laughed at a house that looked like it could have been in that Chevy Chase *Christmas Vacation* movie, which started them talking about which Christmas movies were the best. When they got back to Ford's house, Annie made hot chocolate with amaretto. They settled back on the sofa for the last game of the day.

It was a perfect Sunday. Ford didn't talk about any changes that might be coming at work, and Annie didn't talk about Nick Carlton's death. By the time Ford walked her and Chester back to her apartment that night, Annie was feeling content with the world and its workings, or at least she was until Ford kissed her good night.

"Hey," he said as he came out of the kiss, "I'm going to have to go out of town for a few days."

"Oh," Annie said, "why's that?"

"Just for work."

"But you were just out of town for work." Annie hated the slight whine in her own voice.

Ford smiled at her, but it was a pitying smile, which only made her feel worse. "I have to work, Annie."

"I know that, but why can't you stay stateside?"

He sighed. "Because that's not really my wheelhouse. I've been here too long already."

She nodded. "Right. Of course." The words came out of her mouth, but she felt as if a stranger was saying them. What she wanted to say was *"What the hell does that mean?"* But she didn't.

Ford kissed her forehead. "I should get going. I really need to pack."

He slept at his own house that night.

ANNIE LAY IN BED, STARING at the ceiling for a long time. She hated that Ford would be leaving tomorrow and that she had no idea where he was going. She often wondered how much time would pass before she would find out if something ever happened to him. She knew Boo and Ollie would call her, of course, but she wouldn't be the first to know, the way she would if she was his wife instead of his girlfriend. That never used to bother her, but lately, it started to seem ridiculous that they'd been together so long without any sort of official commitment. For all intents and purposes, they'd been together almost their entire lives. The thought that they might not end up together left her with a hollow feeling. Even imagining life without Ford was difficult.

On the other hand, imagining a different life with him was also difficult. The idea of him as a husband and a father seemed almost comical. That picture was just as hard to put together as the one without him in it at all. Prior to the shooting, Annie's drive and ambition had centered around the police department. When she thought about her future, she'd tended to think about work, but now, she found herself thinking more and more about her personal life. She didn't think her professional life didn't matter anymore—being a good private investigator was important to her—but work no longer superseded everything else.

Monday morning arrived clear and bitterly cold. It matched Annie's mood perfectly. After taking Chester for a long walk, she spent the rest of the morning doing preliminary work on a series of background checks for a local telecommunications company. She liked to get all the computer work out of the way before she did face-to-face interviews. Knowing someone's digital footprint ahead of time helped her formulate better questions for friends and neighbors. Annie prided herself on going above and beyond on the background checks, and the strategy had paid off. This company was the third that had contacted her for assistance.

She was standing in the kitchen eating a peanut-butter-and-jelly sandwich when Celia called.

"I've got a roast in the Crock-Pot," she said. "Want to come out for dinner?"

Annie looked down at the sandwich in her hand. "Yes, please."

"Great, six o'clock?"

"I'll be there."

"Yay!" Celia said. "See you in a little while."

Annie hung up in a much better mood. The prospect of dinner with Celia improved her whole day. She decided to run a couple of errands before her rehab appointment.

Unfortunately, Dawn Sullivan, intrepid reporter, was waiting in the parking lot outside Annie's apartment. This time, Sullivan was dressed for the cold in a heavy parka and snow boots. She looked as though she'd been waiting there a while. Annie gritted her teeth and tried to decide whether continuing was smarter than retreating to her apartment.

"Hi," Sullivan said.

"Are you stalking me now?" Annie asked as she got her keys out of her pocket.

Sullivan ignored the question and stepped in front of Annie's car. "You met with Detective Jansson twice on Saturday."

"You're in my way," Annie said, trying to remain calm, not raising her voice.

"You two used to be partners, right?"

Annie decided to try to defuse the situation with honesty because that was less likely to get her arrested than what she really wanted to do. "We worked together for several years. Sometimes we still hang out."

Sullivan arched a skeptical eyebrow. "Twice in one day? When he's on a major case?"

"What? Don't any of your coworkers like you enough to hang out?" Annie asked.

"Cute," Sullivan replied, but she remained undeterred. "Is it true Laura Carlton hired you to follow her husband?"

Annie kept her expression neutral and said nothing.

Sullivan sighed. "The police haven't been very forthcoming with details about this case."

"Weird," Annie said. "It's like they don't discuss active investigations."

Sullivan ignored the sarcasm and continued. "You and Detective Jansson had a very high close rate. It would make sense if he was consulting with you on a difficult case." She paused, waiting for Annie to reply. "Of course, it would also make sense that you're a suspect if you were following the victim."

Annie felt her jaw clench. She pressed her lips together to keep from telling Sullivan to fuck off.

"Is that it?" Sullivan asked, a twinkle in her eye. "Was he interviewing you?"

Annie glared at her as she pressed the button on the key fob that unlocked the driver's side door. She stepped around Sullivan and got in the car.

"Detective," Sullivan said.

Annie ignored her and put the car in reverse. The backup warning beep seemed to indicate to Sullivan that the interview was over, and she wisely stepped out of the way.

AFTER STOPS AT THE pet store and the post office, Annie walked into the Loudoun Rehab Center for her afternoon appointment.

"Annie!" Kesha said with a big smile.

"Hi, Kesha. How's it going?"

"Pretty good. You can go on back. He's ready for you," she said from behind the reception desk.

Annie stepped through the door at the back of the waiting area to the large room of equipment that looked like a strange gym with massage tables.

Tim Robbins, her physical therapist, approached with a smile. "Hey, you're moving around pretty well today. How are you feeling?"

"Good," Annie said.

"Excellent," Tim said. "How's the leg?" He looked down at his notes on the tablet he was holding.

"It still gets stiff occasionally but better in general."

"Are you doing your exercises and the stretching?"

Annie gave him a half-hearted smile. "Yes on the exercises, not as much on the stretching. I know I should. It just slips my mind."

He affectionately wagged a finger at her. "You've got to stay on top of that."

"I know."

"Okay, well, why don't we stretch you out some first, and then you can go through your exercises. What time are you seeing Carol?"

Carol was the occupational therapist that Annie saw specifically for her hand. She worked at the other end of the room but scheduled her own patients since she worked at two locations.

"I'm not today," Annie replied. "There's something going on at her kid's school, so I won't see her until next week."

"Okay," Tim said with a smile. "So you're all mine." He was perpetually cheerful and positive. Tim had to be in his thirties, but he maintained his straight blond hair in a little boy's cut with bangs spilling over his forehead and a persistent cowlick that wanted to stand up at the crown of his head, so he looked much younger.

"Okay," he said, "up you go."

Tim patted the massage table, and Annie dutifully lay down on her back. He picked up her right leg, and they went through a series of stretches they'd done dozens of times before. Tim made small talk as he stretched her leg. They both loved video games, so that was the topic they explored most often. Physical therapy was strangely intimate compared to other medical interactions, which were often brief and formal. She was always there for at least an hour, often longer, and someone she didn't really know touched her, leaned over her, and even hurt her. The experience was weird, but it was working, which was all that mattered.

When she'd first started therapy, she couldn't put weight on her injured right leg. Now on good days, she barely had a limp.

"You know," Tim said, "I'm going to have to graduate you here pretty soon. I think a couple more weeks, and you might be done with me."

Annie looked up at him. "Seriously?"

He nodded. "Yep."

"Wow," Annie said. The journey to this point had been a long one. "That would be great."

"Now, I don't speak for Carol," Tim cautioned, "so don't get too excited. She might not be done with you anytime soon."

"Right," Annie said, flexing her right hand. "But still, shaving an hour off my appointment every week will be great."

"What will you do with all that free time?" Tim asked, bringing her leg back down to the table.

"I don't know. The possibilities are endless," Annie said, smiling.

Tim laughed. "Okay, you're done here. Go do your exercises, and I'll massage that leg when you're done."

The next half hour was a series of exercises on various machines around the room. No one had to walk her through the process anymore, so she moved along at her own pace. As she lifted weights, she tried to watch CBSN because it ran on several screens mounted on the walls around the room. The difficulty with doing the exercises on her own without a therapist there to chat with was that her mind wanted to wander back to the shooting that had landed her in this place. Pushing those thoughts away was easier with another person to grab her attention. It was more difficult with only a television to focus on.

To make things worse, the news was lame. Some celebrity she'd never heard of had been arrested in LA for driving drunk, and all the talking heads were speculating on how that would affect his career. Annie couldn't care less, and despite her best efforts to resist it, her thoughts strayed back to the events of the shooting.

She was still unable to get past her arrival at the scene. Gunnar had had a joint-task-force meeting that day in Fairfax, so she and Sam Davis had gone out to interview the mother of Eli Ribber, a suspected meth dealer who was linked to a stabbing in the western end of the county. Annie and Gunnar had been working the case with the Loudoun County Sheriff's Department because the meth was being distributed in Leesburg, but the stabbing had happened in Lucketts. The meth dealer was awaiting arraignment in county lockup. He was one of five children and not one of his mother's favorites.

The last thing Annie remembered was walking up to the front door. She knew what happened next because she'd been told and had read the report, but in her mind, she just walked up to that little white house with the peeling paint and crooked screen door over and over and over again. She couldn't help wondering if she'd missed something, some indicator that the front door would be opened by a crazed meth head with guns blazing. The meth head was Theodore Price, aka Tiny, which was a joke. Tiny was six-four and three hundred pounds. He actually told the officers who eventually arrested him that he was only taking meth to lose weight.

Ah yes, Annie had thought, *meth will help you lose weight and your teeth and your mind. What a great idea.* Tiny had come to his dealer's mother's house looking for a fix. Of course, she didn't have anything for him, so he was slapping her around when Annie knocked on the front door.

She sighed and couldn't help cataloging the resulting injuries.

The first bullet had gone through her right hand and into her right thigh but thankfully hadn't hit the femoral artery. Otherwise, she would probably have died. The second bullet had left a deep groove in the right side of her skull and sent shock waves through her brain, causing bruising, bleeding, and swelling. The latter was the real problem because swelling tissue has nowhere to expand inside the skull.

She woke up with remarkably few deficits, considering. She felt as if a brick was jammed in the right side of her head, and the left side felt empty. Her speech was thick and slow, but she could speak, which was something of a miracle. For months, everything had moved in slow motion around her. She could remember how to read but couldn't concentrate enough to do it for very long. Playing video games made her nauseated, and even watching television was challenging because following a story was impossible. She watched a lot of home-improvement shows and other programs that didn't have a plot. Eventually, life returned to normal speed.

"So, what do you think about the *Far Cry* games?" Tim was asking as he walked over to where she was finishing with the weights.

Annie snapped back to the present. "I like them, but I wish they had more options for character development."

"Yeah," Tim agreed. "You kind of get what they give you on that. Let's massage that leg so we can get you out of here."

Annie smiled. "Sounds good."

CHAPTER NINE
Monday Evening

When Annie arrived home from rehab, the light on her answering machine was blinking. She decided to shower and change before she listened to the messages.

Refreshed, she hit the play button.

"You have ten new messages," the answering machine informed her.

Nine of them were from reporters. She erased those.

The last message was from Ford. "Hey babe, I'm being held at work. I'll call your cell later when I can talk." She was irritated that he would leave a message on her home phone instead of calling her cell or sending her a text. She would have gotten rid of her landline a long time ago except Joey knew that number and couldn't seem to memorize her cell number. She was afraid to drop it in case he needed her in an emergency. Ford seemed to use the landline as a convenient way to get credit for calling without actually calling. Frustrated, she erased his message, too, and headed to Celia's place. Sullivan was, thankfully, nowhere to be seen.

Annie parked behind Celia's ancient Land Cruiser and let Chester out of his crate. She'd barely opened the car door when he bolted to join the dobermans, who were running toward the car. The dogs slipped under the fence and ran to the barn. Annie followed them through the horse gate, careful to latch it behind her, and found Celia sitting on the sofa in the tack room with her laptop open and a pile of receipts next to her.

"Hey, girl," Annie said.

"Oh, hi. I thought that might be you. I heard the dogs bark."

"What're you up to?" Annie asked.

"Just putting receipts in the spreadsheet."

Annie smiled sympathetically and flopped down on the other end of the sofa. "Fun."

"Oh, yes, it's loads of fun. There's nothing like watching every dime to make for a good time." She stuck out her tongue in disgust. "The house needs a new roof."

"That sucks." Annie was thankful that her grandparents' house shouldn't need a new roof for several years. Like Annie, Celia had inherited her house from her grandparents. While Annie rented out her grandparents' home for the income, Celia chose to live in hers, so while she didn't have a mortgage, something always seemed to need repairing, between the house and barn. Annie kept an account with a percentage of the rent money to handle repairs, but she rented the house through a broker who managed all that for her. Doing that was a lot easier than what Celia had to deal with.

"Yeah, well, I've had it repaired twice," Celia was saying. "It's just reached the end of its lifespan. I can't put it off much longer. I should have done it earlier in the fall, but I didn't have the money. Now, it can't wait."

"Oh, sorry."

"Me too." Celia looked up from the laptop. "So what's up with you?"

Annie sighed. "Nothing, really. I've got this stupid reporter stalking me. Ford's acting weird. I don't know."

Celia closed her laptop. "That sounds like kind of a lot."

A basket of clean towels for the horses was sitting on top of the dryer. Unable to sit still, Annie got up and grabbed a towel and started folding it.

"So what's the deal with the reporter?" Celia asked.

"She's looking for info on Nick Carlton's murder."

"Shouldn't she be asking the police about that?"

Annie put the towel on the stack with the others. "Yes, but she knows that I found the body and that I used to be a cop and that I was working for Laura Carlton at the time of his death."

Celia let out a low whistle. "Awkward."

"Very," Annie said, picking up another towel. "But I'm handling it. Eventually, she'll go away."

Celia leaned back against the sofa. "Okay, so what's the deal with Ford?"

Annie stopped folding and just looked at the towel in her hands, an old beach towel with little faded blue boats all over it. She remembered it as one Celia had used on a spring-break trip they'd taken to Myrtle Beach in college. "I think he might be going back overseas."

"Oh." Celia pursed her lips in an expression Annie knew meant she didn't want to comment.

Annie frowned at her. "Try not to be too upset about it."

Celia's eyes slid away from her gaze. "You want some dinner?"

Annie sighed. "Yes." She knew Ford was not Celia's favorite person even though Celia had never said as much. Her friend could speak volumes without saying anything.

They walked back to the house, the dogs trailing behind them. The house was a small white 1930s bungalow that was far more modest than the barn, which had been refurbished and expanded several times. With the exception of paint colors, the house remained essentially as it had been when she inherited it. Clearly, most of Celia's interest lay in the horses.

They left their shoes on the porch and walked into the kitchen. Annie loved Celia's house. It was so perfectly Celia. The tiny kitchen was painted sunshine yellow. Strings of garlic and dried herbs hung from the cabinets, which had glass panes in the doors to show off Celia's handmade pottery.

Celia opened the slow cooker, and the delicious aroma of cooked beef filled the room. Annie set the table while Celia took the pot roast, potatoes, and carrots and arranged them on a platter.

"I'm going to make a quick gravy," Celia said, "while the meat rests."

Annie couldn't help smiling. She never made gravy, and meat never got to "rest" at her house. She wasn't even sure what that was supposed to accomplish. Celia, though, always took time with food even if just the two of them were eating. Annie would have taken the Crock-Pot, set it in the middle of the table, and skipped the gravy. She was pretty sure Celia never stood over the stove eating Kraft macaroni and cheese out of a saucepan either.

Annie took a seat at the kitchen table. She smiled to see the electric candles in the windows for Christmas. On the barn doors, she'd seen pine-bough wreaths that were clearly handmade. A Christmas tree stood in the corner of the living room, which was decorated mostly with ornaments Celia had also made. None of the crafts were Pinterest fails. All of them looked as though they belonged at a high-end craft boutique. Annie wished she were in the mood for Christmas. She hadn't even bothered with a tree this year, and she really needed to do her shopping.

The newspaper was on the table, so Annie browsed it while she waited for Celia to finish the gravy. The paper was already starting in on the police department for not solving Nick Carlton's murder, even though only a few days had passed. A murder in Leesburg was big news. Despite the recent surge in population, it was still a relatively sleepy town, and the local papers were wringing every drop out of the story. They mentioned Gunnar and implied that, as the head of the investigation, he should be doing more. Annie felt terrible for him. She knew he was doing everything he could, but the paper made it seem as though he was sitting around eating doughnuts and scratching his head.

Unfortunately, a second article by Dawn Sullivan mentioned that Annie was connected to the case. The article didn't say a lot, but it implied a great deal. Annie had to give Sullivan credit: she knew just how to word things so that, depending on the frame of mind of the person reading the article, they would come away from it thinking either that Annie and Gunnar were having an affair, that he was collaborating with her on the case, or both. Worse yet, the article featured a picture from when she was still on the force.

"Great," Annie said, as she refolded the newspaper.

"Anything good in the paper?" Celia asked as she brought the gravy boat to the table.

"Is there ever?"

Celia shook her head. "Wine?" she asked.

Annie nodded, and Celia poured them each a glass of pinot noir. Annie told her about the articles, including what was implied in the one about her.

Celia frowned and started putting the food on the table. "Well, that's just reprehensible. I'm sure no one will be fooled by that. Everyone knows how the press loves to sensationalize and create scandal where there isn't one."

Annie couldn't help smiling. "I think you're very optimistic about the way other people look at the world. Not everyone is as reasonable as you are."

Celia sighed and sat down. "You might be right. Did I tell you Alan Parker called me?"

Annie knew Alan from when she had been on the police force. He was the head of the Loudoun County Animal Shelter.

"No. What did he want?"

"Someone left two alpacas tied to the fence by the animal shelter."

"What a crappy thing to do."

Celia waved a hand in disgust. "Some people are assholes. Anyway, he says they're in fairly good shape, a little thin maybe. He asked if I wanted them."

"What did you tell him?" Annie asked, although based on the excited expression on Celia's face, she already knew the answer.

Celia spooned roast beef and vegetables onto a plate and handed it to Annie. "I told him I'd take them. I've actually wanted alpacas for a while now, but when the craze happened, the prices shot up so high I couldn't afford them. I think it would be fun to card my own wool and spin it."

Annie was often bewildered by Celia's definition of fun. She was also somewhat perplexed that an alpaca craze had ever occurred. "If you say so."

Celia fixed her own plate and smiled. "I have that little paddock out front with the shed on it. They could live there quite comfortably." She looked at Annie, assessing her. "You know, you might actually like carding or spinning. They're both very soothing."

Annie rolled her eyes. Nothing about carding or spinning sounded soothing to her.

"What? You need a hobby."

Annie laughed. Celia had been telling her she needed a hobby every couple of months for years. "I have a hobby."

"Playing *World of Warcraft* does not constitute a hobby."

"I don't play *WoW*. I like single-player games," Annie said, knowing that would make no difference to Celia. Actually, she was somewhat amazed that Celia knew about *World of Warcraft* at all.

"Whatever. Those are games. That's different. You need something creative to do, something to keep your hands busy."

"My hands are fine just the way they are," Annie said as she flexed her stiff right hand. "Well, mostly fine, anyway. Besides, working the game controllers helps my dexterity. You're not roping me into this wool business."

"It's not a business. I'm not planning on trying to sell the fiber. I just thought it would be nice to knit wool that I carded, spun, and dyed myself."

"You lost me at knitting. I don't have that mysterious third hand that knitting requires."

Celia sighed. "You always say that. I just wish you had something outside of work to focus on. Especially now."

Annie shrugged. "I like work."

"But what about your free time?"

"I own my own business. I don't have a lot of free time."

Celia frowned. "I'm serious."

"Honestly, most of my free time is still spent at PT."

"Physical therapy is not a hobby," Celia said.

"No, but it has been like a part-time job although I might graduate in the next couple of weeks, and then I'll only have to do occupational therapy for my hand."

"That's great!" Celia said.

"Yeah, I'm—" Annie's cell phone rang. She looked at the number. Laura Carlton was calling.

She looked apologetically at Celia. "I'm sorry. I've got to take this." She hit the answer button. "Annie Fitch."

"Ms. Fitch, would you be available tomorrow to meet with me and David?"

"Possibly, what time?"

"Would eleven o'clock work for you? We could meet at my house."

"Let me just check." Annie paused for a few seconds to consult an imaginary calendar. "Sure, I can make that work as long as I'm out of there by one."

"I don't think that'll be a problem," Laura Carlton said.

"Okay, then I'll see you tomorrow."

Celia was looking at her when she hung up the phone. "What was that about?"

"Laura Carlton wants me to meet with her and her lawyer."

"About what?"

"I'm sure it's just to establish a timeline for when I was with Laura, what she hired me to do, standard stuff."

"Really?" Celia asked, her brow wrinkling with worry.

"Yeah, they're probably trying to figure out if I'll be a witness for the prosecution or if they can use me for the defense. That is, if Laura ends up in court for Nick's death, although I'm sure they won't actually say that."

Celia's eyes widened. "Do you think she murdered him?"

Annie shook her head. "No. I don't, but the spouse is always a suspect until they're ruled out. Laura's attorney is just getting his ducks in a row so he's prepared in case she's arrested. It's not a big deal. Don't worry about it."

Celia looked worried. "I don't like that you're involved in this. It seems dangerous. I like it better when you're just doing background checks."

Annie cleared her throat. "Okay, first, I'm not really involved, so I'm not in any danger. And second, background checks may pay the bills, but most of the time, they're really boring. At least this has been interesting, and frankly, it's been nice to see Gunnar again." She took a bite of roast.

Celia eyed her for a long moment.

"What?" Annie said around a mouthful of beef.

"How is Gunnar?"

"Fine."

"Huh," Celia said. "I always liked him."

Annie frowned. "He's married."

Celia looked offended. "I said I liked him as in 'he seems like a nice guy,' not as in 'I want to date him.' Good grief."

"Uh huh." Annie took sip of wine. She knew exactly what Celia had meant, and it didn't have anything to do with Celia wanting to date him. She knew Celia preferred Gunnar to Ford, not that she would ever encourage Annie to date a married man, but more as an example of the type of guy she thought Annie should be with. But Celia, being Celia, never actually said that, so telling her to mind her own business was impossible.

FORD was asleep on her sofa with a basketball game on TV when Annie got home. She sighed. She wanted to still be mad at him, but that was hard when he was so cute and she wouldn't be seeing him for a few days. Annie picked up the remote and turned it off.

Ford sat up bleary eyed. "Hey, where have you been?"

Chester jumped onto the sofa and sat in his lap.

"I ate dinner with Celia. When did you get back from work?"

Ford yawned and looked at his watch. "About a half hour ago."

"Oh." She didn't really want to talk about his job, not that he would anyway. "Have you eaten? Celia sent leftovers home with me." She held up a foil-wrapped paper plate.

"Oh, that's great," he said, getting up and reaching for the plate.

"I can warm it up for you," Annie said. "It'll only take a minute."

"That's okay. It's fine cold." He pulled the foil off and picked up a chunk of carrot and popped it into his mouth.

She smiled at him. "Suit yourself."

He grinned around a mouthful of carrot. "This is delicious."

Annie laughed. "Celia's a good cook."

"A genius," he said.

"You have gravy on your chin," Annie said, still smiling.

"Come here and give me a kiss," Ford said, moving toward her.

Annie laughed, backing away from him. "Get away," she said playfully.

She let him back her up all the way to the bedroom.

CHAPTER TEN
Tuesday Morning

F ord left early the next morning, and Annie spent the beginning of the day curled up on the couch with her laptop while Chester slept at her feet. She'd managed to get a contract with a local recruiting firm to handle all their background checks for potential employees. Some of the checks were extensive, almost enough to qualify for a security clearance. Other jobs just required a quick check for debts, warrants, unpaid child support, and the like. They were easy money and, for the most part, could be done from her living room.

Interviews were more fun, though, so she also contracted through a larger firm to interview friends and neighbors of people who'd applied for actual security clearances. That required some travel, but she always enjoyed interviewing people, seeing their homes, and hearing about their connections to the applicant.

At ten o'clock, she closed her laptop and stretched the fingers on her right hand. Having to do that several times a day was annoying, but she knew that if she didn't, her hand would be stiff and difficult to use by nightfall. After working through her hand exercises, she stretched out her leg and then got in the shower to get ready for her appointment with Laura.

She had an extra half hour before she had to leave, so she went back to the little laundry room/storage closet next to her bathroom and retrieved the cardboard box labeled "Christmas" from the shelf above the dryer.

Annie had decided to skip a tree this year. It would take up too much room in her apartment and require too much furniture be moved around. She plopped a stuffed Santa on the counter between the kitchen and the living room. Then she hung a wreath made of jingle bells on the front door and surrounded her front window with tiny LED lights. The final touch was a woven Nöel door sash she'd received as a Secret Santa gift when she was still a cop. She hung it on the doorknob and pronounced herself ready for Christmas.

"I'll be back, Chester," she said cheerily as she locked the door behind her.

A few minutes later, Annie pulled into Laura Carlton's driveway and put the car in park.

Laura answered the door even before the sound of the doorbell had died away.

"Come in," she said, ushering Annie into the living room.

No Christmas decorations had been put up in this house. Laura looked tired. Her face was drawn, and she was fuzzy around the edges, not quite put together, although she'd clearly made the attempt. Her hair was starting to stray from its bun, and her clothes didn't hang quite right. She looked as though she'd lost weight recently, and she didn't really have any to spare, which left her looking gaunt.

"Have a seat," Laura said. "Can I get you anything? Coffee, tea?"

"No, I'm fine." Annie smiled as she sat on one of two dark-brown sofas across from where David Cohen sat on the other. "What can I do for you?"

"I don't know if you know this," Laura said, "but the police think I killed Nick."

"The spouse is always a suspect," Annie said.

"I told her that," Cohen said.

"I understand that," Laura said, looking from one of them to the other. "But it appears I'm the only suspect, and since I didn't kill him, I have a problem with that."

Annie nodded. "I can certainly understand, but I don't think you're the only suspect. I was talking to the lead detective on the case, and it sounds like they're interviewing a number of people."

"Women," Laura said, grimacing. "You mean women."

Annie didn't say anything. No point in confirming and adding to Laura's already considerable pain.

"I know that my husband fooled around. He was addicted to sex. He has been since I've known him." She glanced away, clearly embarrassed by the admission.

"If you've known about his affairs for years, then why the sudden desire to divorce him?" Annie said. "I'm sure that's what the police are wondering," she added, trying to soften the question.

Laura Carlton closed her eyes and took a deep breath. "Because he was cheating on me."

"I don't follow," Annie said. "I thought you said..."

When Laura opened her eyes, they were glassy with tears. "I didn't care about the hookups. I knew he belonged to that website. I didn't like it, but I knew he couldn't help it. He was always safe, and he always came home to me. He loved me. At least until recently."

"Okay," Annie said. "What changed? And why didn't you mention this when you hired me?" She looked at David, who flushed with embarrassment.

"I should have said something," he said.

Laura came to his defense. "I asked him not to. Honestly, I didn't think it was relevant. I hired you so I would have proof, something I could point to. That's why I kept you watching him even though I had more than enough evidence to divorce him. I wanted to confront him with proof that he was seeing someone else intimately. I wanted multiple pictures of that woman. I couldn't care less about the others. I just wanted him to stop seeing her because he was distant, preoccupied. He didn't have time for me, and that was very unusual. This may sound crazy to you, considering his proclivities, but we were always very close." She frowned and worried at the wedding ring she still wore. "But I wasn't going to continue putting up with his behavior if he had actually fallen in love with someone else."

"Okay." Annie wasn't sure she understood that kind of thinking at all, but she could at least follow Laura's logic.

"And then he was killed." Laura's voice cracked, and a tear slipped down her cheek.

David Cohen rested a comforting hand on her forearm.

"I'm sorry for your loss," Annie said, still unsure why she was there, "but I'm not—"

"My regular investigator for this type of work is tied up with another matter for the firm," David Cohen interjected. "Laura suggested we talk to you. She was pleased with your previous work."

"You want me to investigate Nick's death?" Annie was torn between being thrilled with the additional work, which could lead to more work with Cohen's firm, and being completely flabbergasted that Laura wanted her to investigate a murder. That wasn't really private-eye territory, at least not until an actual arrest was made and a trial date set.

"Yes," Laura said.

Annie leaned back on the sofa. She wasn't sure how to respond. The phone rang, and Laura left the room to take the call.

"I have no desire to get in the way of the police," Annie said quietly to Cohen.

"I don't want that either," he said. "I've tried desperately to talk her out of this, but she wants to be sure all avenues are being pursued. Laura trusts you."

"The lead detective is a good cop," Annie said, "and this is the only open homicide in Leesburg right now. It'll likely be the only homicide in Leesburg this year. It's not like anyone's going to give up on it and let it go cold."

"I understand that," David Cohen said sympathetically, "but the police have to interview everyone, and Laura thinks you can be more precise than that."

Annie thought about the picture of the woman who seemed nice, the one Nick Carlton had seen twice the week she followed him. "Maybe," she said. She was torn. Saying no risked not getting additional work from Cohen's firm in the future, and she wasn't in a financial position to turn down work anyway. On the other hand, this was very shaky ground for a private investigator.

Laura said goodbye to whoever had been on the phone and came back into the living room a few seconds later. "That was Eddie, Nick's business partner. He's very sweet. He checks in every day." She sat back down on the sofa. "Will you help me?"

"I'll see what I can find out," Annie said, "but I'm not in the business of hiding evidence from the police. That's a great way to lose your license in my line of work, not to mention it could land me in jail."

Laura leaned forward and looked into her eyes. "I'm not asking you to. I didn't do this. Nicky may not have been perfect, but he was my husband, and I loved him. Somebody murdered him. Find out who. And when you do, tell the police so they can arrest him."

Annie nodded, taken aback by the fierce look in Laura's eyes. "I'll do my best."

"Thank you," Laura said, standing. Annie watched as she walked back into the kitchen.

Annie and Cohen discussed a fee schedule while they waited for Laura to come back. After a few minutes, Cohen stepped into the kitchen.

A moment later, he came back into the living room. "I think she took the back stairway up to her bedroom," he said.

"I guess she's done with us today," Annie said, surprised that Laura would just disappear like that.

Cohen nodded. "She's had a hard time holding herself together."

"It's good of you to be here for her," Annie said, wondering why Cohen was so attentive and compassionate, which weren't attributes commonly associated with divorce lawyers. Given that he didn't seem the warm and friendly type, she had her suspicions as to why he was so caring toward Laura.

Cohen smiled as though he knew what she was thinking. "To be honest, I'd generally stand my ground more firmly with a client, but Laura and I go back a while. We serve on the boards of several charities together."

Annie understood. "It's hard when a client is also a friend."

David nodded. "I've always been sympathetic to her plight. I knew Nick in school." He wrinkled his nose in disgust. "I'm afraid some people never change. None of this could have been easy for Laura. Her mother is flying in from Connecticut this evening. I'm hoping that will help." He gathered up his briefcase and walked with Annie to the door.

"I'll get right on this. If I find anything, I'll let you know, but I'll also inform the police."

He nodded. "I understand. If you can't get a hold of me, leave a message on my cell. A friend of mine is having his anniversary party at our hunting lodge, and the cell service up there is dicey."

Annie arched an eyebrow and took in his immaculate suit. "You hunt?"

Cohen laughed. "Yes, but you know Loudoun. You make the best old-money contacts on horseback."

Annie nodded. "I hear that."

He opened the door for her, and they stepped out into the late-afternoon sunshine.

"Have a good day, Miss Fitch," he said as he crossed to his Mercedes.

"You too," Annie said as she walked toward her Prius.

CHAPTER ELEVEN
Tuesday Afternoon

Annie came home to Chester waiting in an otherwise empty apartment. Ford had left at five o'clock in the morning. He had an early flight out of Dulles to somewhere. She had a vague memory of him kissing her forehead before he left.

"Come on," she told Chester. "Time for our walk."

She decided to go the long way around town on the off chance that Dawn Sullivan or one of her contemporaries was lurking downtown. The air wasn't too cold, and the wind wasn't blowing, so she thought now would be a good time to clear her head. They meandered through neighborhoods until Annie found herself back at the Old Stone Church. Gunnar was parked by the gate and walking among the gravestones. She knew she had to tell him about Laura Carlton's request that she look into Nick's murder. She sighed. *No time like the present.*

"Hey," Annie said, following Chester into the graveyard. "What are you doing out here?"

Gunnar hunched his shoulders and stuffed his hands deeper into the pockets of his wool overcoat. "I'm supposed to be on my lunch break."

"The nearest restaurant is a couple blocks that way," Annie said, pointing toward Loudoun Street.

Gunnar sighed. "I know. I just thought I'd walk through here again. Trying to find something that looks like a clue, I guess."

"Any luck?"

"Not a bit." He looked up at the sky, where gray clouds were starting to roll in. "Looks like we might get more rain."

Annie looked up. "I think it's just supposed to be cloudy today." She looked at him. "I take it the case isn't going well."

"That would be an understatement. The case isn't going anywhere. Or rather it's going everywhere, which is just as bad. Why would the killer leave the murder weapon here? What's significant about this place?"

A light breeze rustled the dried leaves in the graveyard, swirling them around the headstones. Chester continued nosing around as much as the leash would let him.

Annie shrugged. "I don't know. Maybe he was on foot, and this was on the way home."

"I considered that, but it doesn't help us much." He waved his hand toward all the houses beyond the cemetery. "We've got suspects that live in that direction, but so far they've all got alibis."

"I thought you liked the wife for it."

"I thought so, too, but we can't get anywhere with her. He had a life-insurance policy worth a million, but around here that isn't that uncommon. Actually, it's kind of low, considering their combined income. I can find plenty of witnesses that saw them argue but no one who can put her in Leesburg after the time that she says she left. She says she went home to an empty house, so no proof of that either. She parked her car in their garage, and none of her neighbors noticed her coming back. Not to mention, this cemetery isn't anywhere near the restaurant where they ate, and it's in the wrong direction to go back to her house. Even if she went out of her way, this headstone is too far from the road for her to have just thrown the rock out of her car window, which means she would have had to park the car again and walk it over here. That doesn't make any sense."

Annie nodded. "True. To be honest though, Gunnar, I've never been able to see her clubbing Nick in the head with a rock, anyway. It's just not her style. What about the women from the website. Any luck there?"

Gunnar sighed. "I've interviewed thirteen women so far who had lunchtime trysts with him, Stan and Dave have interviewed a dozen each, and we've got dozens more to go, but I think that's a dead end. He was on that website for two years. Those women don't know him. It was quick, anonymous sex. They didn't even know his name, much less his address and habits. Except his sexual habits."

"Classy," Annie said. "What about the partner?"

"Eddie Peabody. The night of the murder, he was at Leesburg Beer Company. A waitress confirmed it although she said it was crowded that night for the game, so she couldn't give me exact times for his arrival and departure. She said he came in sometime before the game started and left sometime after it was over, but she couldn't swear he was there the entire time."

"And Nick didn't come in?" Annie asked.

"She didn't think so but wasn't positive. Apparently, Nick and Eddie meet there all the time to watch games, so it blurs together for the waitress, but the bigger problem with the partner is no motive," Gunnar said. "As a matter of fact, he's terrified he's going to lose work. Apparently, Nick Carlton was the face of the company and brought in most of the clients. The business is healthy right now, though, so I don't see an issue there. I've got forensic accountants looking at the books, but so far it's all legit."

"That's tough," Annie said. "Any possibility it's just a random mugging?"

"It's looking more and more like that, but I really hope that's not it. The town council is going to go apeshit if this is random. I've got about a million newspeople breathing down my neck. Yesterday, a blogger called me for a quote. A fucking blogger. What's that about?"

Annie smiled. "Brave new world. But you can't really blame them. A murder where the tourists shop is big news. If it helps, I've got a reporter stalking me now too."

He looked at her, a pained expression in his eyes. "I know. I saw the article. Not what I need right now."

"Don't worry," she said, patting his arm. "It's not like I told her anything."

Chester had apparently decided he was bored of sniffing the same ground over and over. He came and sat down on Annie's foot.

"It doesn't matter. There's nothing to tell, so they'll just imply whatever they want."

She squeezed his forearm. He looked more tired than he had the other night. She knew the pressure of this case was taking its toll.

"I know," she said. "I actually have some news. I'm not sure if you'll think it's good or bad."

"Okay," Gunnar said, drawing out the word. "What?"

"Laura Carlton hired me this morning to solve her husband's murder." Annie winced as she said it, knowing he wasn't going to like it.

The conversation hit a long pause while Gunnar just stared at her, clearly flabbergasted.

"Gunnar?" Annie asked.

"Yeah. Look, Annie, as much as I'd love to have you on this case, I can't have you interfering with an active investigation."

Annie sighed. "I told them that. I told them I wouldn't interfere and I wouldn't withhold evidence even if it pointed at Laura."

Gunnar's eyebrows rose in surprise. "And they still hired you?"

"Laura is convinced she's your only suspect, and she says she didn't do it. She wants me to find out who did."

"You know she's not our only suspect."

"I told her that."

"This could just be a smoke screen," Gunnar said. "I mean it's not like the fact that we used to be partners is a secret."

"Maybe it is a smoke screen," Annie agreed, "but I can't afford to turn down the work, so I just wanted you to know."

"I appreciate the heads-up." He sighed.

"I promise you'll know everything I know."

He blew out a frustrated breath, clearly unhappy. "Fine," he said. "I'm going to go by the station and then start in on more interviews."

Annie smiled at the information as though they were still partners and he was keeping her up to date on his whereabouts. She wanted to tell him to give himself a break, but she knew he couldn't. "Make sure you pick up some lunch on the way," she said.

He nodded, and she watched him walk back to his unmarked car. She and Chester slowly walked back to her apartment. The snow was mostly gone, and what was left was just dirty rows on the outer edges of the sidewalks.

ON the walk back home, Annie thought about the photographs she'd taken of Nick Carlton's many women. Back at the apartment, she sat down at her computer and pulled them up. She printed the pictures she had of the woman with the sweet face, the one he'd seen twice the week she'd followed him.

She tucked them into the folder behind the other pictures before examining the woman's image again. She was blond, shorter and heavier than Laura, but she had a real twinkle in her eye and a kind, open face. She looked to be about Nick's age, give or take five years. Annie thought about the two meetings she'd photographed. Unlike the other women, this one didn't meet Nick at a hotel. The first time they'd met had been at a busy restaurant in Sterling on a Friday afternoon. He'd held her hand through lunch, but they'd driven off in separate cars. Afterward, he'd returned to work and gone home as usual.

The second meeting was a couple days later. They'd met at an office building and kissed before going inside. Annie had that all on film. Unfortunately, a janitor pushing a large cart prevented Annie from getting inside in time to follow them onto the elevator. The elevator stopped at several floors, so Annie had no way of knowing which one they'd gone to. She remembered the frustration of losing them. The building was a typical mixed-use office building, with an architectural firm, several doctors, a couple of law offices, and a dentist. Annie really wished she knew whom they were there to see. They left the building all smiles, kissed again, hugged for a long time, and then left in separate cars. Nick stopped and bought flowers before driving straight home.

Annie shook her head. All the other women she'd photographed him with had been obvious hookups. They'd met around noon at various hotels around Loudoun, mostly on the eastern end of the county. The women were all dressed for office work, and they hurried out of the rooms as though they had to get back to it. Neither Nick nor the women looked caught up in the afterglow of those encounters. Instead, they seemed as though they'd brokered successful business deals. At the time, she hadn't realized the sweet-faced woman was different. Annie had been focused on gathering evidence about his affairs, but now with the benefit of hindsight, she could see that Nick's relationship with the sweet-faced woman was not like the others at all.

She considered how she was going to go about identifying the sweet-faced woman, whom she'd christened the SFW. Annie thought it unlikely that she was part of Nick's hookup website, but if she was, Gunnar would know who she was soon enough.

She spent the afternoon cyberstalking Nick Carlton to see if she could see the SFW in photographs of him anywhere on the internet. Nick and Laura were very active in Loudoun County community activities. They were both part of Rotary and the Chamber of Commerce and either together or separately sat on the boards of several charities. Photographs of Nick and Laura were plentiful online. Unfortunately, the SFW didn't appear in any of them, even when Annie looked in the backgrounds of all the photos, carefully searching for her face. She lost track of time until Chester pawed at her leg. She'd been on the computer for hours. The apartment had gotten dark around her. She turned on a light and looked at Chester.

"Okay, buddy. Enough work for today."

CHESTER wanted to go out, so they took a walk.

"Don't find anything interesting," she told the little terrier. "I've got enough on my plate now thanks to you."

He ignored her and sniffed happily along, but to Annie's relief, he didn't find anything. Unfortunately, Dawn Sullivan was walking up King Street as Annie and Chester were walking down Market. Annie instantly regretted avoiding the alley where she'd found Nick's body. If she'd gone down the alley, she would have missed the reporter.

"Good evening, Ms. Fitch," Sullivan said cheerily, as if they were old friends.

"It was," Annie said.

Sullivan's smile broadened. "Don't be like that. My sources tell me that Laura Carlton has hired you to look into her husband's death."

Annie was taken aback, confused as to where Sullivan was getting her information. Despite her surprise, Annie held her tongue.

"Look," Sullivan said. "Like it or not, you're a bit of a local celebrity since the shooting."

Annie's jaw clenched.

"You being involved in what could turn out to be the biggest crime of the year is big news. Now, you can talk to me, or you can let me speculate based on what I do know. It's your choice, but I'd like to proceed with balanced facts. On the other hand, I'm getting a lot of pressure from my editor to stay on top of this story. The TV networks may be over it, but we're not. So, absent details, I'll run with what I've got and let people draw their own conclusions."

Annie blew out a frustrated breath. "You do that," she said and kept walking.

When she and Chester got back to her apartment, she made a big pot of coffee and a peanut-butter-and-jelly sandwich before sitting down at her laptop again.

She'd done a Google search for photographs of Nick Carlton and hadn't found any of the SFW, so she decided to try Facebook. Nick wasn't particularly picky about who saw his pictures and his friends list. Unfortunately, the SFW wasn't among them. Annie was hoping they knew each other in some other capacity outside the affair and the woman with the sweet face might be tagged in one of his photos, but she wasn't that lucky.

Frustrated, Annie cleared off her coffee table so she could spread out everything she had on Nick Carlton. When she had been a cop and they were stumped, they used to stick photos of the people involved in a case on a big board in ops and look at it to try to make connections. Chester jumped up on the sofa and sat next to her. He looked at the coffee table, too, as though also trying to find something she'd missed. Maybe he would—he'd certainly found plenty in the case so far.

She considered the location of the body. Chester had found Nick behind Susan's Sundries. Maybe Nick was having an affair with Susan or one of her staff. She made a note to check whether Gunnar had interviewed them. Also, the murder weapon had been left in the Old Stone Church graveyard, which might or might not have been significant. She knew she was grasping at straws, but at the moment, she didn't have anything else to grasp.

She called Gunnar.

"Hey, Annie," he answered. "What's going on? Has your dog solved the case?"

She laughed. "No, not yet. But he appears to be working on it."

"Great. Could you tell him to hurry it up? I'd like the weekend off." He sounded tired and grumpy.

"I've been trying to find that woman Nick met twice the week before he died. The one you said looked nice."

"Any luck?" Gunnar asked.

"Not yet. Did you ask the business partner if he knew any of those women?"

"Yeah," Gunnar said. "He said he didn't."

"Okay. I figured you'd already asked. I just wondered if he knew this one, though. You were right. She's different."

"Yes, she is. We've managed to identify the others you photographed because he met them on the website. Speaking of which, guess how many women Nick Carlton had for lunch."

"I don't know, fifty?"

"Try four times that."

"He had sex with two hundred women?"

"Two hundred twelve, to be exact. He's been on that website for years. He's part of their Golden Cock Club. He once won a contest so that he and three women could join the mile-high club in a private jet."

Annie rolled her eyes. "Oh, good grief."

"Yeah. And over a third of the two hundred twelve are currently married. Half of the rest have boyfriends, and a couple of them have girlfriends. I'm up to my eyeballs in suspects."

"What a nightmare."

"Tell me about it."

"Did you already interview the people at Susan's Sundries?"

"Stan did. It's just Susan and two other women, one full-time, one part-time. I have their names around here somewhere. Susan has been out of town on vacation for over a week, and the other two said they didn't know Nick."

"Okay. Have you found any connection to the Old Stone Church?"

"Not so far."

"This case sucks," Annie said.

Gunnar chuckled. "Now you know why I was wandering around the cemetery this morning."

"Well, if I find anything, I'll let you know."

"Please do."

"Yep." She started to hang up.

"Annie?"

She put the phone back to her ear. "Yes?"

"It's nice working with you again."

Annie smiled. "It's nice working with you again, too, Gunnar."

She hung up the phone as a key turned in her door lock. Chester jumped off the sofa and barked madly.

Ford cracked the door open and poked his head in. "It's just me, buddy," he said, leaning down to pet Chester. He looked up at Annie. "Is this a bad time?"

Annie sighed. "No. Of course not. Come on in."

He stepped inside closing the door behind him. "You look kind of stressed."

Annie stood on her tiptoes and kissed him. "I'm okay, but Laura Carlton called this morning and hired me to find Nick's killer."

Ford scowled at her. "What are you talking about? The police handle murders. Leave it to them."

Annie didn't like his tone. "She feels like the investigation is primarily focused on her. I told her I didn't think that was the case, that the police were looking into all possibilities, but she didn't believe me."

"You think she's trying to get you to cover for her?"

"No. I told her I wouldn't and that I'd pass on anything I found to the police. She hired me anyway. From the beginning, I didn't think this was her, and I still don't, but if it is, I won't hesitate to tell the police. She knows that."

He frowned. "I don't like this. It's dangerous."

Annie rolled her eyes at him. "So noted. It's a paycheck. It's not like I can afford to turn down work."

His frown deepened as he looked down at the coffee table. "Is this the case?"

"Yeah, or my part of it, anyway."

"Why do you have a picture of Jenny Tomlin?"

Annie perked up. "Which one is that?"

He held up a picture of the sweet-faced woman.

"You know her?"

"Yeah," he said, looking at the picture. "She was a year ahead of me at County."

"That was a long time ago. You sure that's her?"

"Yeah, she was a cheerleader. We dated for a while. Sweet girl. She was also a hell of a gymnast. Very flexible. You should see what she wrote in my yearbook."

"Something sexy, I suppose."

He grinned. "Oh yes."

Annie rolled her eyes. "You sure this is her?"

"Her hair is different, and she's a little heavier now, but yeah, that's definitely her. Why do you have her picture?"

"Nick Carlton met with her twice when I was following him."

"Weird." Ford set down the photo. "Small world."

"Very," Annie said, picking up the picture of Jenny Tomlin. She was pretty in that all-American-girl way, corn-fed and healthy, blond with a big smile, the kind of woman everyone liked. Even in her thirties, Jenny managed to project a youthful air.

"Did she and Nick date in high school?"

"Not that I know of," Ford said. "But Nick went out with a lot of girls, so maybe."

Annie looked back at Ford and arched an eyebrow at him. "Flexible, huh?"

Ford grinned at her. "Very."

Annie shook her head. "You're terrible."

"I only have eyes for you now, baby."

Annie laughed. "You always had eyes for me."

He plopped down next to her on the sofa. "True."

"You want to get some dinner?"

Ford looked away from her. "I can't. I got the call. I need to pack and get out of here. My flight is in a couple of hours."

Annie's smile faded. "Oh. Can I ask where you're going?"

"You can ask," Ford said, giving her a weak smile. "But I can't answer."

"Right." Annie sighed.

"I just wanted to see you before I left." He kissed her softly on the lips before getting up and walking back to the bedroom.

Annie sat on the sofa and watched him go. She closed her eyes and took a deep breath. She'd known this day was coming, but she wasn't really ready for it to be here. She'd purposefully avoided thinking about it, and now that it was happening, she was completely unprepared. She let out the breath slowly and walked to the bedroom.

"Can you tell me how long you'll be gone?" she asked.

Ford looked up from the heavy canvas duffel he kept under the bed. "Six weeks, maybe a little more. Three months at the absolute outside."

"Three months?" she said, shocked.

He gave her an easy smile. "It's really not likely to be that long. Six weeks is probably all I'll need."

She frowned at him. "To do what?"

He stopped packing and walked over to her and wrapped her in a hug. "To do what I do. I love you. You know that, but this is my job."

She pressed her face against his chest and breathed him in, the faint scent of bay rum mixed with his own warm smell. She loved that smell and would miss it terribly. She didn't want to cry, but a tear slipped down her cheek anyway.

"It's going to be okay," he said softly. "You're fine now."

She nodded into his chest.

After a moment, he let her go and went back to packing, which took him only a couple minutes. "I've got to finish getting what I need at my place." He reached into his pocket and pulled out a set of keys.

"They're sending a car for me. Do you think you could drive the 4Runner some while I'm gone and check on my place?"

She nodded, not trusting herself to speak.

He leaned down to kiss her again, clearly meaning it to be quick, but she gripped the front of his shirt and kissed him deeply, passionately, with the all the emotion she couldn't express in words. When she finally let him go, he touched her cheek before slipping out of the room. Annie didn't walk him to the door.

When she heard the door click shut behind him, the tears fell. Before, she had never cried when he left. Being overseas was part of his job. She understood that, but after the shooting, after having him home most nights for the last year, she didn't want him to go. Her chest tightened, and a wave of panic washed over her with a deep-seated sense of dread that he wouldn't return. She took a deep breath and used the calming technique she'd learned in therapy after she'd been shot. She counted five things she could see, four things she could taste, three things she could hear, two things she could smell, and one thing she could feel. After a few minutes, the panic subsided, but the sadness remained. Chester sat at her feet, looking at her. She scooped him into her arms, kissed his head, and went back into the living room.

THE pictures were still spread out on the coffee table. Annie blew out a long, slow breath and pushed aside her feelings about Ford's departure. She couldn't do anything about that, but she could work. She picked up Jenny's picture and wondered if she was married. Maybe an angry husband had killed Nick. Statistically speaking, that seemed pretty likely.

She opened her laptop and returned to Facebook. Jenny Tomlin turned out to have a popular name. Seventy-three women on Facebook had that name, and Annie sorted through them all. Finally, she found the right woman, thankful that the right Jenny Tomlin wasn't terribly security-minded. She left photographs and her basic information public. The photos proved Annie had the right woman, and the information let her know that Jenny Tomlin was living in Falls Church, Virginia, a mere forty-minute drive from Leesburg. Using a phone-book website, she got an exact address. She lived in an apartment complex off Wilson Boulevard on the Arlington border. Annie looked at the place on Google Street View and realized she knew it well. A high-school friend of hers used to live on the same road. She called the phone number and confirmed that Tomlin was home. She considered calling Gunnar but decided to wait. The lead could turn out to be a big, fat nothing. On the other hand, he had been trying to identify Jenny Tomlin as well, and he'd probably be pretty pissed with Annie if she did the interview without him. Annie dialed his number.

Gunnar picked up on the first ring.

"I've got an ID on the sweet-faced woman," Annie said without preamble.

"Really? Who is she?"

"I'll tell you on the way to the interview."

"Annie..." Disapproval was audible in Gunnar's voice.

"This is a courtesy call, Gunnar. You can come, or I can tell you what I've learned afterward. Your choice."

"Dammit. I can't go right now. We're on our way to interview a husband of one of the women Nick had for lunch."

"You like him for this?"

"He's got a record for aggravated assault."

"Sounds promising," Annie said.

"God I hope so. I'm already sick of this case. Go do your interview. I'll do mine, and then we'll meet and compare notes," Gunnar said.

"That works for me."

Annie changed into a more professional outfit, kissed Chester on the head again, and headed to Falls Church.

CHAPTER TWELVE
Tuesday Evening

Annie was going against the bulk of the traffic as she drove to Jenny's apartment, but the roads were still congested. The drive to Falls Church took over an hour this late in the evening. The apartment complex had several open parking spaces. Apparently, a lot of residents weren't home from work yet. Annie hoped Jenny would still be there. She hadn't given her any information when she called. She just asked for her, and when she answered, Annie had hung up.

Annie got out of the car and stood next to the locked security door, rifling through her purse as though she was looking for keys. Not much later, a man came out, and she caught the door and slipped in. He didn't look twice at her. She took the elevator to the sixth floor, found apartment 612, knocked on the door, and was delighted when it opened.

"Jenny Tomlin?" Annie asked.

"Yes?" Jenny was dressed casually in yoga pants and a T-shirt, but a pair of sensible pumps sat on the floor next to a black leather tote.

Annie handed her a business card. "I'm Annie Fitch. I'm here to talk to you about Nick Carlton."

All the color drained from Jenny's face. "Uh..."

"May I come in?"

Jenny paused for a second before stepping back from the door. "Sure," she said.

Despite a basket of clothes in the middle of the living room floor, the apartment was cozy and inviting. Annie couldn't help but draw a contrast between Laura Carlton's gigantic beige McMansion and this charming little place. Jenny Tomlin liked rich colors, and photographs and paintings reflected her life and interests. A bookcase was over-flowing with books and DVDs. The whole place was tidy but lived in. Had she been Nick Carlton, Annie knew where she'd have preferred to spend her time.

"I'm sorry," Jenny said, indicating the basket of clothes. "I was just going to start some laundry. Would you like a cup of coffee?"

"That would be great," Annie said.

"It'll just take a minute. Have a seat."

Annie sat on the denim sofa. A small bar separated the kitchen from the living room. Annie realized that Jenny might not know Nick was dead or that she might even have killed him, but looking around, Annie didn't think so. Anyone was capable of murder under the right circumstances, but Jenny didn't seem the type that could club a guy in the back of the head with a rock and leave him to die in an alley. That seemed like a man's way to murder, and she wondered if they weren't wasting their time interviewing all these women. Maybe Gunnar would hit the jackpot with his aggravated-assault guy. Still, Jenny might not be at all what she appeared to be, so she still had to be interviewed.

Jenny kept her back to her as she prepared the coffee, so Annie could see the tight set of her shoulders.

"When did you last speak to Nick?" Annie ventured.

"Not for a couple of days," Jenny said, handing Annie a cup of cof-fee. "Do you need cream and sugar?"

"Black is fine," Annie said.

She hesitated. Jenny clearly didn't know Nick was dead, but if An-nie told her now, she wasn't likely to get much information.

"So you know Nick well?" Annie asked.

Jenny bit her lip. "Yes." She didn't meet Annie's eyes. "Did his wife send you?"

"In a manner of speaking," Annie said.

"I need to sit down." Jenny sank into a deep purple wing chair as if her legs could no longer support her.

Annie noticed a certain roundness to Tomlin's belly and that she wasn't drinking coffee. She decided to risk a rude question. "How far along are you?"

Jenny lowered her eyes as though she'd been expecting the question. "Fourteen weeks. I never meant for this to happen. Honestly, I never thought I'd have children. My first marriage didn't work out, and it just didn't seem likely I was going to meet anyone else at this point." She blinked back tears. "And then there was Nick." She looked up, anguish etched on her face. "I didn't know he was married. He doesn't wear a ring. We ran into each other at a party held by a mutual friend. I hadn't seen him since high school, so when he called and asked me out, I said yes." She shook her head. "I never expected it to amount to anything. I mean, I really struggled with whether or not to even tell him I was pregnant. God, to get knocked up at my age. So stupid... It's embarrassing."

Annie nodded sympathetically. "These things happen."

"The thing is he didn't tell me he was married until after I told him I was pregnant. And I thought, 'That's it. He's going to dump me, and I'm going to be stuck on my own.' Every possible panicked thought, you know?"

"Yeah." Annie found herself feeling legitimately bad for the woman.

"But it was weird, he didn't do that at all. He was so excited about the baby. He started telling me how it wasn't working out with his wife and how he loved me, and he wanted to be with me and raise the baby together. We've only been dating a few months and with the married thing... I don't know how to feel. I'm moving to California. My parents live out there now. I'm not brave enough to try to do this on my own. Nick says he's going to get a divorce and sell his half of the business and move out there with me. I don't know whether to believe him or not. He seemed serious, but now that you're here, I guess..."

Annie set down her coffee. "Look, California is a good idea," she said. "But Nick isn't going to go."

"He sent you to tell me, right?" She looked away. "I knew he'd changed his mind when he hadn't called. I can't say I'm surprised."

Annie shook her head. "It's not that. I'm sorry to have to tell you this, but Nick died."

"Oh my God," Jenny gasped, and tears streamed down her face. Annie sat quietly, waiting for her to pull herself together. She thought about other times in her life when she'd had to deliver this kind of news. People's reactions varied wildly. Some sat in stunned silence, some got angry, some laughed because they thought she must be joking, and some burst into tears as Jenny did.

When she could speak again, Jenny gasped, "What happened?"

Annie took a deep breath and blew it out slowly. "He was found in an alley in Leesburg near the town garage. It was the night we got all the ice and snow."

Jenny was still crying. "I don't understand. Did he fall? What was he doing there?"

Annie shook her head. "We don't know. The police are still investigating."

Annie stayed with Jenny Tomlin until she'd calmed down enough to call a friend to come over and be with her. She listened to Jenny extol Nick's virtues: how sweet he was, how he'd encouraged her to go back to school, how excited he was about the baby.

When Jenny's friend finally arrived, Annie offered her condolences again and left. On the drive back home, Annie tried to fit the pregnancy into the puzzle of Nick Carlton's death. The pregnancy in and of itself didn't mean much, but whoever knew about it might make all the difference in cracking the case.

THE drive home took considerably longer than the drive into Falls Church. As she crawled along in traffic, Annie called Gunnar.

"Jansson," he answered.

"You done with your interview?"

"Yeah, how'd yours go?" he asked.

"Weird. Want to grab some dinner and compare notes?"

"Sure. Where?"

"How about Leesburg Brewing Company in an hour?"

"Great. See you then."

Annie had just enough time to change into jeans and a sweater and run Chester out for a quick potty break before she met Gunnar.

He was already sitting at a small table by the window with a dark amber beer in front of him. The restaurant was busy, so Annie had to thread her way through the crowd to get to his table.

"Hey," Gunnar said when she sat down. He waved at the waitress, who nodded that she'd seen him.

"So how'd your interview go?" he asked.

"You first," Annie said.

Gunnar let out an exhausted sigh. "It could have been great. The guy was a solid wall of racist tattoos, and he referred to his wife exclusively as 'that slut.' The more he talked, the easier it was to see him clubbing just about anyone in the head with a rock."

"I sense a 'but' coming," Annie said.

"*But* the night Nick Carlton was killed, this guy was sleeping it off in the Montgomery County Jail. Already confirmed it."

"Crap," Annie said sympathetically.

"Yeah, so what about you?" He took a sip of his beer.

"Somewhat better." Annie slid the photo of Nick with Jenny Tomlin across the table toward him. "Ford identified her. He said she was a year ahead of him in high school. They briefly dated. Her name is Jenny Tomlin, and she's pregnant with Nick Carlton's baby."

Gunnar let out a low whistle. "Wow. That's interesting. Could be our motive."

The waitress appeared then and set down two menus. "Can I get you something to drink?" she asked Annie.

Annie pointed at Gunnar's beer. "I'll have one of those. And a cheeseburger with sweet-potato fries."

The waitress looked at Gunnar. "I'll have the same but with regular fries," he said.

"I'll be right back," the waitress said as she picked up the menus.

Annie smiled. "Thanks." She turned back to Gunnar. "The question is who knew about the pregnancy, and would anyone other than Laura Carlton care?"

Gunnar leaned back in his chair. "Maybe this woman killed him. I mean he doesn't exactly seem like the stand-up type."

"That's the funny thing. He told her he was going to sell his half of the business, leave his wife, and move to California with her."

Gunnar looked doubtful. "Really?" He took another sip of beer. "Of course, if he did, it would upset his business partner too."

"Or he was lying." Annie said. "Maybe he had no intention of following her out to California and only said that to encourage her to go. Who knows? Either way, she seemed legitimately shocked when I told her he was dead."

"So we're back to the wife. Or maybe the business partner."

"Or a random killing."

Gunnar frowned. "You're just saying that because you're working for the wife."

Annie shook her head. "That's not true. Nothing about this seems like something she would do. If he had been cleverly poisoned or professionally hit, that would be in keeping with what I know about Laura Carlton. But clubbing him in the head with a rock and leaving him to freeze to death in the street just doesn't seem like her style, and it certainly isn't something a professional would do."

Gunnar shook his head. "No. But I don't believe this is random. It feels personal. A random mugger isn't going to come armed with a rock. He pissed someone off and got clubbed in the head for it. The problem is there are so many players. I've just got to find the right person with a grudge against him. I wonder if Eddie Peabody knew about the pregnancy and whether or not Nick told him he was planning on selling out and picking up stakes."

"Good question," Annie said. "Assuming he was actually planning on doing that. My money says it was an empty promise. I doubt he was planning to go anywhere."

Gunnar ran his fingers through his hair. "Jesus. The guy was up to his eyeballs in reasons to be killed."

"Was he? Or was it the just the same reason over and over? Did he do anything besides have sex with a lot of women who weren't his wife?"

Gunner chewed on that for a bit and sipped his beer. "Did he need to do more than that?"

Annie rubbed her eyes. They felt like sandpaper, a side effect of having cried earlier. "Probably not. Jealousy is definitely one of the top reasons to murder someone."

The waitress arrived with their food.

Gunnar looked at Annie. "So what are you going to do now?"

"I think I'll go talk to Laura Carlton in the morning, tell her about the pregnancy, and see how she reacts."

"Mind if I tag along?"

Annie smiled. "I'm sure I can't stop you."

Gunnar nodded as he picked up his burger. "True."

Annie called Laura after dinner while they stood outside the restaurant. She agreed to meet with them at eight o'clock the next morning.

When Annie hung up, Gunnar said, "So I'll pick you up at seven thirty tomorrow."

"Sounds good."

CHAPTER THIRTEEN
Wednesday Morning

The drive to Beacon Hill down Route 7 prompted Gunnar to start on what his fellow officers always referred to as "the boring tour." He waxed nostalgic about the days when the scenery on the drive west out of Leesburg was filled with farms. "We went on a wine tour down there last year," he might say, or "I dated a girl that lived off this road." The other police officers found that irritating whenever they rode with him, but Annie had always kind of liked it. She found Gunnar's deep voice soothing and his narration almost like a chant, and as a result, she had a wealth of information about all the inconsequential moments of Gunnar's life in Loudoun County.

When Laura opened the door, she looked more rested than the last time Annie had seen her.

"Thanks for coming," Laura said. "You have news?"

"Yes," Annie said. "You know Detective Jansson."

Laura glanced at Gunnar and nodded before walking into the living room and taking a seat on the sofa. A toilet flushed in another part of the house, and a few moments later David Cohen appeared and took a seat on the other end of the sofa.

Annie sat across from them in one of the velvet wingback chairs. Gunnar took the other.

"I appreciate you taking the time to meet with us this morning," Annie said.

Laura nodded. "Of course."

"We just have a few questions," Gunnar said.

"All right then," Cohen said.

"Did Nick ever mention divorce to you?" Annie asked.

Laura shook her head. "No."

"So you two hadn't discussed it?" Annie said.

"No. I wanted to have all the information at hand before I approached him. To be honest, I thought there was a chance, well..." Laura didn't continue the thought and folded her hands in her lap, but she'd clearly been hoping Nick would change his ways.

"Okay." Saying what she needed to was more difficult than Annie had anticipated.

"What did you find out?" Laura prompted, her fingers clenched tightly in her lap as if she were steeling herself for the answer. Gunnar sat silently, waiting for Annie.

Annie could do nothing but say it. "It appears that Nick had a relationship with a woman that resulted in a pregnancy."

Laura gasped and pressed her fingers to her mouth. Tears began to fall. "Oh God. That makes so much sense."

"What does?" Annie asked.

"A baby. Nick always wanted children. We've spent tens of thousands of dollars over the last couple of years for fertility treatments, but none of them worked for me. Oh God." She put her face in her hands and began to cry in earnest. Her shoulders shook with sobs.

Another woman came into the living room. She looked like an older version of Laura. She was sedately dressed but completely accessorized.

"What's happened?" she asked, clearly alarmed by the scene in front of her.

"Mom." Crying, Laura went to her mother, who wrapped her in a comforting hug.

Laura's mother glared at them.

David Cohen shifted uncomfortably in his seat.

Annie and Gunnar glanced at each other. Words didn't need to be exchanged between them, and they stood in unison.

"I'm sorry," Annie said to Laura Carlton's mother.

"We'll see ourselves out," Gunnar said.

Laura's mother nodded at them while Laura continued crying in her arms.

When Gunnar opened the door for them to leave, Eddie Peabody was walking up the sidewalk. He was a small, slim man who kept his graying brown hair slicked back, revealing a high widow's peak. He was dressed in a well-cut suit and tie and was carrying a covered casserole dish. Annie understood his impulse. Some mysterious instinct drove people to bring over copious amounts of food whenever someone died. They couldn't help themselves. She and Gunnar exchanged somber hellos with Eddie.

"Just so you know, she's pretty upset," Gunnar told Eddie. "Apparently, Nick got another woman pregnant recently. Did you know anything about that?"

Eddie's face fell. "No. Poor Laura. Things just keep getting worse."

"You didn't know anything about the pregnancy, then?" Annie asked.

"No. Nick never said. My God, she must be devastated. I'll just drop this off and go. At least her mom is here now."

Annie and Gunnar nodded in awkward agreement.

"Either Laura Carlton deserves an Academy Award, or she didn't know about Jenny Tomlin's pregnancy," Annie said as she got into Gunnar's unmarked cruiser.

"Yeah. That looked legit to me. Dammit," Gunnar said, starting the car. "That wasn't how I wanted that to go. Although we may have another break," he said, looking at his phone.

"What's that?"

"I just got a text from Mike. Someone tossed Carlton's wallet in the entrance of a police station in DC. They found it this morning, so presumably, it was dropped off sometime last night."

"Seriously? That's weird."

"Yeah," Gunnar said, backing out of Laura's driveway. "Like we're supposed to think what? That some scumbag from DC drove all the way out to Leesburg to mug Nick Carlton with a rock in the middle of a snowstorm and then felt so bad about it he returned the wallet to a police station?"

"Someone is trying to divert your attention and muddy the waters," she said, smiling.

Gunnar snorted. "You think?"

Annie laughed. "Well, at least you know for sure it wasn't random now."

"And someone is panicking out there," he added.

"Seems like it. Because if that was part of a plan, it's a pretty weird one," she said.

"Yep," Gunnar agreed. "And panic causes mistakes."

"Hey, can you drop me off on the corner? I want to get a bottle of wine," Annie said as they approached Loudoun Street.

Dawn Sullivan was walking toward her as she got out of the car.

"Crap," Annie muttered under her breath, but Gunnar had already pulled away from the curb.

"Good morning," Dawn Sullivan said. "How did your meeting with Detective Jansson go?"

"Stop stalking me, Sullivan," Annie said.

"Who's stalking? I just saw you get out of his car."

"Yeah," Annie said, walking in to the Leesburg Vintner. "He gave me a lift."

"To the wine shop?"

"Yep," Annie said, but she knew how bizarre that sounded even as she said it.

Sullivan followed her into the store. "I haven't been in here yet," she said.

"No?" Annie said, with faux interest. "It's great."

"Hi, Annie," said Mike, the owner, from behind the counter.

"Hey, Mike, have you met you Dawn Sullivan? She just moved here. She works for the paper." While Mike asked Dawn where she was from, Annie grabbed a bottle from the reasonably priced reds bin and took it to the counter.

"Good choice," Mike said, as he rang it up. "This just came in. So what do you like to drink?" he asked Dawn.

While Dawn talked white versus red with Mike, Annie slipped out and hurried home.

ANNIE'S PHONE BUZZED in her pocket as she walked toward her apartment.

"Hey, how are you doing?" Celia asked.

"I'm okay. Tired. I didn't sleep that well last night. I'm going to try to get in a quick nap."

"What's up? Why didn't you sleep? You know you need to stay rested. The doctor said—"

"I'm fine. It's just Ford went back overseas for work, and he's going to be gone for at least six weeks."

"Oh," Celia said. "I'm so sorry, sugar."

"It's okay. He had to go back sometime. I'm fine," she repeated. "So what's up?"

"I have two tickets to the Loudoun County Chamber Music Association's Christmas fund-raiser. Want to be my plus one?"

"Really? Why do you have tickets?"

"Because Marc and Gary are members, and they go every year. Except this year, Marc has a conference in Key West, and Gary is going to go with him. They're going a few days early to get in some fun and sun. I think Marc is trying to make up for the whole LA debacle."

"That wasn't really his fault, was it?"

"Of course not, but you know what a baby Gary can be. It's easier just to placate him. Anyway, they offered me the tickets in exchange for farm-sitting."

"Great. I'll go, then."

"It's dressy. Do you have something to wear?"

Annie frowned. "I have nice clothes."

"I know, but have you tried them on lately?"

Annie hadn't. She hadn't been really dressed up since she'd been shot. She wondered if any of her dresses fit right anymore. "I'll try them on. If nothing works, I'll go get something."

"Well, you'll have to get something today or tomorrow because it's tomorrow night."

"Crap."

"The Key West trip was sudden."

"I'll see what I can do."

Celia squealed. "Yay! I'll see you tomorrow night, then. I'm so excited."

"Okay."

"Come on," Celia said. "It's been ages since we went out together. It'll be fun."

"I know it will."

When Celia hung up, Annie went back to her apartment to assess the clothing situation. It wasn't good. She tried to think of the last time she'd been really dressed up. She was pretty sure it was Neil Hellman's wedding, and that was four years ago. She and Ford occasionally went out but never to anything too fancy. She had three cocktail dresses to choose from. After trying them on, she had zero dresses to choose from. She'd lost weight but not in a good way. She looked more frail than slender. Her dresses gaped unattractively and sagged where they should have been supported. She was going to have to go shopping. She looked at the clock. Shopping wouldn't be any better tomorrow, so she saw no sense in putting off the inevitable.

ANNIE TOOK TWO HOURS to find a dress that she could afford, that was appropriate for the charity function, and that looked decent on her. She missed the tone her body used to have and vowed to start lifting weights again. After she'd been shot, she wasn't able to lift more than a few pounds for a long time. That restriction was over, though, and she really needed to get back to working out.

Irritated with her own laziness but pleased to have a dress that fit, she left the outlet mall and went to Puccio's, where she picked up two egg-salad sandwiches and a big garden salad to share with Miss Mabel for a late lunch.

Miss Mabel was happy with the salad. "I only ever get greens when one of you girls come. Them boys never bring greens."

Annie chuckled. "Typical."

Miss Mabel and Annie chatted about some new construction that was supposed to be happening in town, although zoning issues and complaints of bullying from previous tenants who'd lived on the property seemed to have stalled the whole thing.

After lunch, Annie walked over to Eddie Peabody's house on Princess Street. It was a large, two-story Georgian home with a one-story addition in the back where Nick and Eddie had their office. It was painted gray and had white trim and maroon shutters. The house and yard were lovingly maintained.

She stopped across the street and stood looking at it for a moment before walking around to the office entrance. That was Wednesday afternoon, so Eddie might have been working. The door opened into one large room, painted a deep red, with dark wooden wainscoting. A large Oriental rug covered most of the floor, and heavy, dark crown molding topped off the room. The entire effect was one of old-money confidence designed to make you trust these men with your investments. A small, elegant desk by the door was empty, as was a long oxblood leather sofa along the wall.

Eddie was sitting behind one of two large mahogany desks, staring at a computer monitor. The desk on the other side of the room was empty except for a picture frame and a cup of pens. Presumably, that was Nick's desk, and the police had taken his computer.

Annie cleared her throat.

He looked up, startled. "Oh, I'm sorry, my receptionist is off for the afternoon. What can I do for you?" he asked, standing and reaching for his sport jacket.

"Hi," Annie said, walking toward his desk and sticking her hand out. "I don't think we've ever been formally introduced. I'm Annie Fitch. I see you around town all the time, and we saw each other briefly at Laura Carlton's house yesterday."

He gave her a look as if trying to place her as he pulled on his jacket. "Yes." He lightly shook her hand.

"I don't know if she's mentioned me. I'm doing some investigative work for her." She gave him one of her cards.

"Oh." Eddie's brow furrowed. "No. I don't think she said anything about that. When I saw you at the house, I assumed you were a cop."

Annie smiled. "I used to be. I work privately now. She actually asked me to look into Nick's death."

He raised his eyebrows, clearly surprised at the news. "I thought the police were covering that."

"They are. I'm just doing some adjacent work for Laura."

"Oh," Eddie said. "All right, what can I do for you?"

"You knew about his affairs, right?"

He smiled tightly. "Of course. We were best friends as well as business partners. Don't misunderstand me. It's not like I approved. He never let it interfere with work, so..." He shrugged.

Eddie had an odd, somewhat clipped way of speaking. He paused just a second longer than normal between sentences as if he was being exceptionally careful about everything he said.

"I get that," Annie said. "Do you mind if I ask you some questions about Nick's affairs? If we could narrow this down to some disgruntled husband somewhere, we might be able to take the pressure off Laura and get this whole ugly situation resolved."

"Of course," Eddie said, gesturing to a leather wingback chair in front of his desk.

Annie took a seat, and Eddie settled into his high-backed leather desk chair. It was probably meant to make him seem affluent and powerful, but it looked instead as if it was trying to swallow him.

"So how long have you known Nick?" she asked.

"Since middle school. His parents moved here from Fairfax in the middle of sixth grade." He straightened his laptop to line up with the edge of his desk.

"Wow, that's a long time."

All over the wall behind him were framed photographs interspersed with plaques from various professional organizations, along with Eddie's college degree and CPA license. The photographs all featured Eddie and Nick in various vacation settings. In one, they stood on either side of a huge sailfish, and in another, they were whitewater rafting. One even showed them standing on either side of Tiger Woods.

Annie looked back at Eddie. "I guess you guys were really close."

Eddie nodded and got a little glassy-eyed. "The closest. Best friends and business partners," he repeated. "It doesn't get much closer than that."

Annie smiled sympathetically. "It must be a terrible loss for you."

Eddie nodded. "It's been hard."

"How about Laura? When did she and Nick meet?"

"Freshman year of college. They didn't start dating until junior year. Nick tried earlier, but she knew his reputation. She hung out with us, though. We were all friends. Nick worked on getting her to go out with him the whole time."

"So she knew about his reputation with women?"

Eddie chuckled. "Everyone knew."

"Why do you suppose she agreed to go out with him?"

Eddie shrugged. "She fell in love with him, which wasn't so unusual. A lot of women loved Nick. The weird part was that he loved Laura back."

"But he never stopped seeing other women?"

"He did for a while, at first, but then... I don't know." He shook his head. "It was like he couldn't help himself. He was more discreet after he started dating Laura, and the number of women dropped off considerably. At least until he found that website."

"Did you ever meet any of the women Nick was seeing?"

Eddie shook his head. "No. He would mention them sometimes, just in passing. But once he got on the website, it was pretty much just lunchtime hookups. Not much to talk about unless things got freaky." Eddie grimaced at the memory.

Annie arched an eyebrow. "Did that happen a lot?"

Eddie shrugged. "Not really. Mostly, he didn't talk about it. He'd take a long lunch but then get back to work."

"Nothing sticks out? No time when things got weird or a husband or a boyfriend showed up?"

Eddie shook his head slowly. "Not really. I told the police all this. Nothing really sticks out. I mean, there were some women who were into bondage and stuff like that, which wasn't really Nick's thing, but I guess he was willing to accommodate when necessary." He shifted uncomfortably in his seat. "I could tell it bothered him though because that stuff he would talk about."

"So what was Nick's thing?" Annie asked.

"Just sex," Eddie answered, adjusting his tie. "Nick just wanted sex and a lot of it, and he was willing to do whatever he had to do to get it."

Eddie shifted again in his seat and cleared his throat. "I mean, I like sex as much as the next guy, but Nick was in a whole different league."

"And he didn't try to hide it from you?" Annie found the whole situation bizarre.

"No, but he didn't brag about it either. I mean, he used to, back before he got married, but after a while, he knew he had a problem, like drinking or taking drugs. He knew it, and I knew it. I think it kind of embarrassed him. There wasn't much to talk about."

"Did he ever try to get help? Go to a group or see a therapist or anything?"

Eddie nodded slowly. "Yeah, actually, he mentioned that he might look into a group a couple weeks ago. Although he joked that a sexual addiction group was probably a great place to pick up women, so I don't know how serious he was."

"Do you know if he ever went or which group he was looking at?"

Eddie shook his head. "No. He never said anything else about it."

Annie nodded. "I see. And how about Laura? Did she know?"

Eddie grimaced. "Of course she knew. I mean, not every single incident, and he certainly didn't tell her about the weird stuff, but in general, she knew."

"And she was okay with that? You don't think that's odd?"

"Personally? Yes." He leaned back in his chair and laced his fingers together. "Marriages are funny things, though. It's hard to say what goes on behind closed doors and why people put up with the stuff they put up with. I know it sounds weird, but aside from the cheating, Nicky was a great guy, even a great husband. He really loved Laura, and she loved him too." He teared up again and pulled out a handkerchief to wipe his eyes. "Sorry."

Annie smiled sympathetically at him. "He only ever loved Laura? There was no one else special?"

Eddie gave a half shrug. "No. Not that I know of. Not really."

"Okay. If not special, then how about long-term? Did he hook up with anyone more than once?" Annie was wondering if Jenny was an anomaly or if Nick had other longer-term affairs or even children that Laura didn't know about.

Eddie cleared his throat again. "You know, there might have been someone in town, a few months ago, but I'm not positive."

"Any idea who it might have been?" Annie asked.

Eddie shifted in his seat. "No. He was very private about names."

"How about more recently? Anyone special lately?"

Eddie shrugged again. "I'm not sure. Maybe. I know the website would occasionally hook him up with someone he'd been with before."

"How would he see the same woman through the website? Could he request someone, or could she request him?"

"Maybe, but I don't think so," Eddie said. "I've never been on it, but from what Nick told me, everything was anonymous. He would put in his location and availability, and the website would find him a match, make a hotel reservation, and book him a date with someone who had matching availability."

"He didn't know who would be at the hotel?" Annie asked, shocked by the sheer risk involved.

"I don't think so," Eddie said. "But keep in mind, this service was expensive. It's not like some cheap app. Not just anyone could afford the monthly fee, and not just anyone was accepted. I think they did some kind of background check, and I know he had to have a physical."

"That seems really exclusive, and if the website set up the hotel reservation, I guess it would have to be costly."

"Oh, yeah. That way, the hotel reservations never showed up on his credit card. From what I understand, the whole thing looked like a charity on the statement, but of course he never took it off his taxes," he was quick to add. "They were nice hotels too."

Annie didn't mention she knew that already from following Nick.

Even though Gunnar had already asked Eddie about Jenny Tomlin, she decided to ask him herself. "How about a woman named Jenny Tomlin? Ring any bells?"

Eddie did the slow headshake again. "Not that I recall."

"Really?" Annie said. "I figured you'd know her. She went to County."

"Oh," Eddie said, raising his eyebrows. "You mean the cheerleader?"

"Yes. Did Nick ever mention her?"

"I don't think so," Eddie said. "At least, not recently. He might have said something back then. He probably did. He commented on all the girls."

"Did they date in high school?"

"Not that I know of."

Annie looked at him, trying to gauge if he was lying, but that was hard to tell. He was still teary-eyed, and he kept wiping his eyes and nose with a handkerchief. "Can you think of anyone who might have a reason to kill Nick? A disgruntled client, angry husband, anyone?"

Eddie shook his head. "No. The police asked me the same thing, and honestly, I can't think of anyone. Our clients loved Nicky. He was the one who brought in most of the people who weren't recommended by existing clients. I mean, I can get by on the clients we have, but it's going to be hard to continue to grow the business without Nick. He never missed an opportunity to pitch our services. His dentist invests with us, so does his orthopedist, the guy who runs the car wash, practically everyone he ever met. Everybody loved him." His voice cracked on the last part.

Annie decided to give him a break. "Thank you for talking to me." She stood and handed him her card. "If you think of something, anything, give me a call."

Eddie nodded. "I will."

"I'm very sorry for your loss," Annie said and left him to his grief. She walked by Nick's desk on her way out the door. The wall behind it was empty except for a long shelf. On one side of the shelf, a small framed painting of a foxhunt rested on a decorative easel. Next to that was what looked like a pair of antique dueling pistols in a wooden display box, and next to that was a clear box containing a signed football. The framed picture on his desk turned out to be a wedding photo of Nick and Laura.

SHE texted Gunnar, asking him to call her when he could, and walked back toward her apartment. A few seconds later, Gunnar called.

"I just talked to Eddie Peabody," she told him.

"And how was that?" Gunnar asked.

"He seems really broken up about Nick's death."

"Yeah, he was when I talked to him too."

"What did he say when you questioned him about Jenny Tomlin?" Annie asked.

"He said he didn't know her."

"He told me the same thing," Annie said, "but when I said she went to County, he remembered her being a cheerleader."

"Interesting," Gunnar said. "Did he know Nick was seeing her?"

"He said no."

"Do you think he's lying?" Gunnar asked.

"I don't know," Annie said. "Why wouldn't he say if he knew? He did say Nick might have been seeing someone in town a while ago, but he wasn't sure."

"Yeah, he told me that too. I wonder who that might have been," Gunnar said.

Annie wondered that too. "He also said Nick had mentioned maybe joining a group for sex addicts, but he wasn't sure how serious he was. You guys run across anything like that in his emails?"

"No," Gunnar said. "I went ahead and sent Stan over to talk to the guy who runs the group in Leesburg anyway, but he didn't recognize Nick."

"How about the forensic accountants? Are they turning up anything in the books?"

"Not so far," Gunnar said. "But if there's a motive in there anywhere, they'll find it."

"Anything else come off the wallet?"

"Nope. The tech says the wallet has a pebbled surface that's terrible for prints, and it doesn't look like anything but cash was missing."

"How much cash?"

"Mrs. Carlton said they stopped by the ATM near their house before going out to dinner and Nick withdrew four hundred dollars. He gave her two hundred and kept the rest. She left before the bill for dinner came, so she doesn't know if he paid cash but thought that was his intention. Dinner didn't show up on his credit card, so he probably had a little over a hundred dollars on him when he died."

"That's a good take for a mugging. You think someone saw him pay in cash and followed him out back?"

Gunnar blew out a slow breath. "I don't know. Lightfoot has a pretty swanky clientele. Not likely one of them followed Nick out to steal his cash, and I think the restaurant staff would have noticed some lowlife lingering around, watching how people paid."

Annie pushed her fingers through her hair. "That's true. What about the staff? Anything there?"

"No. Apparently, they were slammed around the time of the argument. No one was on break. Besides," Gunnar continued, "a mugger would have a knife or a gun and would've taken the credit cards too. If it was kitchen staff, they could have easily picked up a knife. This wasn't planned. It was impulsive, which sounds like he pissed off the killer. I've got people trying to trace Laura's movements, as well as Eddie's, on the night of the murder. So far, nothing is sticking to either of them, but I've also got people tracing the movements of all the local women he slept with, as well as their husbands or boyfriends. Several of those guys work in DC, so it would have been easy for them to toss the wallet there."

"Seems like a risky move if you work downtown," Annie said.

"True," Gunnar said, "but people get stupid when they're nervous. I just need something to break, just one thing."

"You'll get it," Annie said, hoping she was right.

When the call ended, she was almost back to her apartment. She wished she could go over the case with Ford. He could be very insightful sometimes, and he knew the players in this game. Thinking about Ford weighed on her heart, so she spent the rest of the day doing errands and chores to try to keep her mind off him and give herself a sense of accomplishment since she didn't seem to be accomplishing much in the way of solving Nick Carlton's murder.

CHAPTER FOURTEEN
Wednesday Afternoon

Annie was putting away groceries when her cell phone rang. She winced when she saw the number. Her father was calling. She'd meant to call him after Joey's party and apologize for having to leave early. "Hi, Dad."

"Annie," he said, his deep voice dripping disappointment.

"What's up?" she said, trying to keep her voice light.

"I was just checking in. You left so suddenly the other night, and when you didn't call..."

"I know. I'm sorry about that. A client's husband was murdered, and the police wanted some photos I had taken of him."

A deafening silence filled the other end of the call. She hadn't meant to tell the truth. A convenient lie about stomach problems or feminine issues would have saved her a lot of grief.

"Dad..."

"What are you doing involved in a murder investigation?" He managed to keep from shouting, but the anger was clear in his voice.

She knew he wasn't really mad at her but just concerned and afraid she'd be hurt again. Unfortunately, he only knew how to express that as anger. She sighed.

"I'm not really involved," she lied. "I just had photos the police needed. It couldn't wait. I wanted to get them the pictures right away and be done with it."

"And are you?"

"What?"

"Done with it?"

"Yes." She took a deep breath and tried to keep calm. "Relax. I'm not a cop anymore. It's fine. It's not like I went looking for this." Annie was grateful the *Washington Post* wasn't running Dawn Sullivan's articles and her father didn't read the Leesburg paper.

"But you're obviously still involved with the police, which can turn dangerous. You need to find another career." He was using his dad voice now, as if she was messing up at school and he needed to set her straight.

"I like my new career," she said, trying not to let irritation seep into her voice.

"Your so-called 'new' career is too damn much like your old career. Why don't you go back to school? I can help with that. You could stay here and go to Marymount. It's just up the road. Or George Mason, that's not far. You already have a bachelor's in communications. There's a lot you can do with that." He'd gone from scolding to pleading. "Maybe there's a master's program that you—"

"Dad, I don't want to go back to school."

"But—"

"Seriously, we can't keep having this conversation. I like being a private investigator. I've been building my client base. Things are going well. Why can't you be happy with that and let it go?"

"Because the last time I let it go, someone shot you in the head."

And now he's brought up the shooting. The circle of the conversation was complete. Annie sighed. She was so sick of this argument. She rubbed at the scar on her head, which had perversely decided to tighten up and itch. "I know. I'm sorry. It's not like that now. I wish you could understand that."

Another long pause hung between them. "I wish I could too."

"I'll be there Friday night for dinner, okay?"

"Okay."

"I love you, Dad."

"I love you, too, Annie. Please be careful."

ANNIE went to lie down. Since the shooting, she'd found she had less emotional fortitude for difficult conversations. Talking with her father had exhausted her.

She didn't want a job in an office somewhere and even thought she might not be able to do that even if she wanted to. Given some of her physical and mental changes since the shooting, the idea of getting up every morning at the same time and going to work whether or not she'd slept well the night before seemed kind of impossible. She was very sensitive to lack of sleep now and needed more of it than she ever had before. Things that were difficult for everyone seemed so much harder now than they used to be. Her doctors had cautioned her that she had to be careful of those issues, but she hadn't realized what a big deal they would be. Even something as basic as missing a few hours of sleep made it difficult to speak clearly or find the words she wanted. When she was tired, she also limped more. Stress or dehydration could cause the same problems.

Having control of her own schedule helped offset some of those problems. The ability to seek work she could handle helped too. Until she'd agreed to look for Nick's killer, she hadn't done anything really stressful. She didn't want to work for anyone else again and let them decide what she would be doing and when. While she missed her coworkers and the regular paycheck, the freedom of setting her own schedule and choosing her own work wasn't just nice, it was almost a necessity.

Explaining all that to her father was hard because that meant bringing up the shooting and how it had changed her. Talking about it pained them both, and she didn't want to remind either of them of what she'd lost that day. Once upon a time, she was sharp, and she had a great memory and a quick wit. Now things were slower. She didn't feel stupid as much as somewhat muted, as if the lines that used to be so crisp and clear were now faded and a little blurry. She took copious notes now because her memory wasn't as good as it used to be, but she found that gave her something tangible to look through as she considered a problem. She had once been known for being quick on her feet, but that seemed to have been replaced by a methodical doggedness.

When she'd first woken up in the hospital, her speech was slower and slurred as though she was drunk. She even felt kind of drunk but not in a good way. Getting off the steroids and the pain medication had helped. Over time, the world around her edged back into focus, her speech cleared, and her mind seemed less foggy. She was reminded of when she was a kid and she would see how long she could hold her breath underwater. Those last few seconds, she'd get a blurred black edge around her vision, then she would pop up out of the water for that clearing gulp of air. However, after the shooting, the woman that emerged from the pool was not the same as the one who'd gone in. She wondered how much of the difference her friends and family saw, but she was afraid to ask.

Her cell phone rang. Thankful for the interruption, she got up and answered it.

"Hey, I need to bring the Land Cruiser into town to be fixed," Celia said. "Can you pick me up and take me back home? I'll be your best buddy."

"You're already my best buddy," Annie said, smiling. "When do you need me there?"

"How about in an hour?" Celia said.

"Okay. Text me if it changes."

Annie put the rest of the groceries away then took Chester for a walk. The day was beautiful, high forties and no wind. They walked through the neighborhoods, avoiding downtown and the possibility of running into Dawn Sullivan.

Annie focused on staying in the moment to push back the anxiety that always accompanied thinking about the shooting. She tried to appreciate everything going on around her the way Chester did. *Oh, to be a dog*, she thought.

CHAPTER FIFTEEN
Wednesday Night

Celia was waiting in front of AutoNation Toyota when Annie pulled up. She looked irritated.

"They tried to talk me into buying a new car. Can you believe that?" Celia said as she got into the car.

"Wow, that's crazy. The Land Cruiser is just... what, twenty years old?" Annie deadpanned.

"Twenty-two, and it's just fine. It needs the occasional repair, that's all."

Annie nodded and pulled out of the parking lot. "Of course."

Celia huffed. "You're as bad as they are. Why is everyone so quick to throw things away? It's ridiculous. There are plenty of Land Cruisers around the world that are still being driven, and they're way older than mine."

Annie suppressed a smile. "Yes. Like all those cars in Cuba."

"Well, those are mostly American cars, but yes."

"If only we lived in a communist state where we couldn't import so much new stuff..."

Celia glared at her. "Now you're just making fun of me."

Annie chuckled. "Yes."

"So do you want to stay for dinner?" Celia asked, smiling.

"Also yes."

"Great, I've got sloppy joes in the Crock-Pot."

"I love you," Annie said.

"Everyone does."

Annie rolled her eyes. "You should figure out how to bottle your self-esteem and sell it."

"I know, right? I'd make a fortune."

"Billions and billions," Annie said as she took the exit toward Purcellville. They both laughed.

DINNER was delicious and followed by an episode of *Wallander*, which Annie hadn't seen, followed by several episodes of *Unbreakable Kimmy Schmidt* to lighten the mood.

As she was pulling out of Celia's driveway, Annie realized she was low on gas. She glanced at her dashboard clock. The time was just before midnight, so she stopped at a twenty-four-hour gas station near Purcellville known for having amazing homemade cookies. Annie felt she deserved a cookie, maybe even two. She fueled up the car and went inside to pay. She remembered she had forgotten to get milk at the grocery store and went to get a carton from the cooler in the back. A tall woman with her long hair pulled back in a blue bandana was getting a Coke out of the cooler.

She recognized Susan of Susan's Sundries from having met her a few months before, when she and Celia had gone into the shop looking for a birthday gift for Celia's mother.

"Susan, right?" Annie said.

"Oh, hi!" Susan said, clearly trying to place Annie as she closed the cooler door.

Annie smiled. "Annie Fitch, I was in your shop a couple of months ago with my friend Celia."

Susan nodded. "Right, right." She was a good seven inches taller than Annie and had auburn hair that was either natural or very expensively dyed. On another woman, the bandana would look ratty, but Susan managed to look self-possessed and strong in it, like Rosie the Riveter. Streaks of paint stained her denim shirt and khaki pants.

"I heard you were on vacation," Annie said. "When did you get back?"

Susan wrinkled her nose and shrugged. "Wow. Leesburg really is a small town, isn't it?"

Annie chuckled. "Some days more than others. I only know because I went into the shop looking for a gift the other day and you weren't there. One of your employees told me you were in the Bahamas."

"Actually, it's been more of a staycation, but I told my employees I was going to the Bahamas so they wouldn't call me. I'm trying to get some serious work done on my house." She held a finger to her lips. "Mum's the word though."

Annie smiled. "Of course. That sounds great. I could use a break like that."

Susan grinned. "I'm getting so much done. I'm telling you, you should try it, and I should get back to it."

"Right. Have a good night." Annie watched from the back of the store as Susan paid for her soda and walked out.

IN the parking lot, Annie called Gunnar.

He answered on the first ring, which told Annie he hadn't been sleeping.

"I'm sorry to call you so late," Annie said.

"That's okay," Gunnar said. "What's up?"

"You'll never guess who I just ran into." She pulled onto the bypass.

Gunnar sighed. "Let's see... Santa, and he killed Nick Carlton over Mrs. Claus."

Annie chuckled. "No. Susan Wright."

"Susan Wright from Susan's Sundries?" He perked up. "She's back in town?"

"As it turns out, she never left."

"Seriously?" Gunnar said, more alert now.

"Yep. She told me that she's on a staycation and that she told her employees she was in the Bahamas so they wouldn't call her."

"That means she might have been around when Nick was killed."

"Yes, it does."

Gunnar let out a low whistle. "Well, isn't that interesting? I wonder what else her employees don't know."

"Want to go ask her in the morning?"

"I'll pick you up at eight," Gunnar said.

"See you then." Annie hung up and continued back to her apartment.

The short drive was marvelously quick when no traffic was around. Back home, she fed Chester and took him for a quick walk before getting ready for bed. As she was falling asleep, she dared to hope they might finally be getting somewhere with this case.

CHAPTER SIXTEEN
Thursday

The next day, Annie woke to the sound of heavy rain hitting the roof. She tried to console herself that at least it wasn't snow, which is what they were getting farther west and north, but that didn't help her mood any. The rain was falling so hard that Chester didn't even want to go out, so she took a big golf umbrella and dragged him outside to do his business.

Gunnar showed up at eight o'clock, and they drove out to Purcellville, where Susan lived.

"You know this isn't strictly kosher," Gunnar said. "I shouldn't be bringing you."

"I didn't have to tell you I ran into her, you know," Annie said. "I could have interviewed her myself first."

"I know that. And I appreciate the call, which is why I picked you up."

Annie watched the windshield wipers sweep away the rain. "I'm glad you see it that way."

"I miss working with you. We had a good close rate, you and me."

Annie smiled. "Yes, we did."

"If I had the money, I'd hire you on as a consultant for this case. We need more officers."

Annie arched an eyebrow at him. "I know the department doesn't have the budget for stuff like that. Besides, I'm working for Laura Carlton."

Gunnar frowned. "There is that."

"You know she didn't kill him."

"Do I? Do you?"

"Yes, on both counts. The longer this goes on, the less it looks like Laura."

"Yeah, I know," Gunnar admitted. "You like Susan for it?"

Annie shrugged. "I don't know. I don't even know if she knew Nick, but she looks like she could club someone in the head with a rock—at least physically. She's probably five-ten or more, and she looks pretty fit to me."

Gunnar chuckled. "Well, I certainly hope she's the killer. And I hope as soon as we knock on the door, she confesses. I can arrest her on the spot, and we're good to go."

Annie smiled. "I hope so too. Then we could get lunch at Tuskie's to celebrate."

Gunnar laughed. "Yeah, that would be great."

SUSAN lived on a beautiful piece of property on the eastern side of Purcellville, about ten minutes from Celia. The house was a two-story Georgian, freshly painted a buttery yellow with black shutters and what looked like a new roof.

Gunnar let out a low whistle. "Nice place."

"Now I can see why she needed a staycation. The maintenance on this place must be extensive," Annie said.

"Worth it, though. I'd love to fix up a place like this someday."

"Even if I had the patience to work on it, I will never have the kind of money it takes to buy a place like this."

"Yeah." Gunnar sighed. "Me either. Where do you suppose Susan's money is coming from?"

Annie shrugged. "I'm not sure. I can't imagine the soap business brings in stacks of cash, but who knows what she did before she moved here?"

"Let's ask," Gunnar said as he pulled the car into the circular driveway in front of the house.

The middle of the circle was filled with what looked like rose bushes, but they were hard to identify in the winter. On either side of the front door were gigantic azalea bushes. Annie was sure they were gorgeous in the spring. They knocked on the door, but no one answered. Eighties music was blasting inside.

Gunnar frowned. "She probably can't hear us over the music, and there isn't a doorbell."

"Let's go around back," Annie suggested.

They followed a crumbling slate walkway around the house and through a rusted iron gate dangling from one hinge. It was set into a wrought iron fence that was barely visible under a heavy curtain of ivy.

"I guess she hasn't gotten to the backyard yet," Gunnar said.

A slate patio sat at the back of the house, desperately in need of replacement. Sagging steps led up to the back door. Annie peeked in. She could see Susan painting. She was a wearing a gray sweat suit streaked with paint, and her hair was tied back in a red bandana.

Gunnar pounded on the back door, and Annie waved. They eventually caught Susan's attention. Startled, she picked up a remote, and the music stopped. She opened the door.

"Hey," she said to Annie. "What's going on?"

"Hi," Gunnar said. "I'm Gunnar Jansson with Leesburg PD. "I'd like to talk to you for a few minutes. Can we come in?"

Susan glanced at Annie again. "Sure." She stepped back from the door, and Annie and Gunnar followed her into the kitchen, which smelled of fresh-brewed coffee and latex paint. The floors were wide old planks, newly refinished, and the walls were freshly painted the light green of a Granny Smith apple.

"Your place looks fantastic," Annie said. "I love this color."

"Thanks," Susan said, gesturing toward a long rustic oak kitchen table. "Have a seat? You want a cup of coffee?"

"That would be great," Gunnar said, pulling out a rail-backed chair.

He and Annie sat at the table while Susan poured them all coffee. She brought it to the table on a tray. The cups were orange porcelain that looked as though they were from the 1970s. Annie thought Celia would love them. A matching sugar dish sat there too, along with a little white cow-shaped porcelain cream pitcher. Susan sat down, and they each took a cup.

"This is a beautiful property," Gunnar said.

"It looks like you've done a ton of work," Annie added.

"Thank you," Susan said, glancing from one to the other. "I have. So what's this about?"

"Nick Carlton," Gunnar said.

Susan frowned. Her jaw tightened. "What about him?"

Gunnar glanced at Annie.

"He's dead," Annie said.

Susan put a hand over her mouth. "Oh God. How?"

"Murdered," Gunnar answered. "I'm surprised you don't know. It's been all over the news."

Susan stared at them. "I haven't been paying attention to the news lately. Who killed him?"

"We don't know," Gunnar answered. "We were hoping you could shed a little light on that."

"Well, I don't know," Susan said, raising her eyebrows. "I imagine it could be any number of people."

"Why do you say that?" Gunnar asked.

"Because," Susan said defensively.

"Because why?" Gunnar prompted her.

"Because he was careless with people's feelings, and he couldn't keep it in his pants," she snapped.

"You knew him well, then?" Gunnar asked.

Susan pressed her lips together in a tight line before answering, "Not as well as I thought."

"You were lovers," Annie said.

"Yes, for a few months until I caught on to his games." She reached for the sugar and dumped a large spoonful into her coffee.

"Were you aware that he was married?" Gunnar asked.

Susan sighed as she stirred her coffee. "Yes. But cheating on your wife with one woman, with whom you are supposedly having a discreet affair, and sleeping with half the county are two different things."

"So he was cheating on you and on his wife," Annie said.

"Yes. And I found that unacceptable."

"Then you were upset," Gunnar said.

Susan looked at him. "Yes, but not enough to kill him, if that's what you're implying. Nick's an ass, but I didn't want him dead."

"Okay," Gunnar said. "Can you tell me why you told your employees you were snorkeling in the Bahamas?"

She gave Annie an acidic look. "I told Annie last night that I wanted to work on the house without interruptions. Joniqua and Ashley are both completely capable of running the shop, but if they know they can get in touch with me, they'll call to run things by me when they don't really need to."

"I see," Gunnar said. "So what were the circumstances of your breakup with Nick Carlton?"

Susan blanched. "I think I need to call my lawyer."

"Susan—" Annie started to say.

Susan held up a hand. "I'm not saying another word. I'd like you both to leave."

"Okay," Gunnar said, standing. He handed her his card. "Have your attorney call to make an appointment to come down to the station, and we can finish this conversation there."

Susan's jaw tightened as she took the card. Her eyes shot daggers at Annie. "Fine. I'll see you to the door." She led them to the front door through a living room covered in drop cloths spattered with paint.

"Thank you for your time," Gunnar said as Susan slammed the door.

THE rain stopped as they walked back to the car. Annie turned to Gunnar. "Well, that was interesting. Man, if looks could kill."

"You'd be very dead," Gunnar said, frowning. He started the car but didn't put it in gear. Instead, he got out his cell phone and made a call. "Did you get it?" he asked the person on the other end. "Really? Okay, then. I'll read it when I get back to the station." He tucked the phone back in his coat pocket and started out of the driveway.

"What was that about?" Annie asked.

"I asked Mike to run a background check on Susan."

"And?"

"And Susan's husband died under mysterious circumstances in the Caribbean two years ago."

"Really?"

"Yeah, charges were never filed, but she was a person of interest for several weeks."

"Wow." Annie had had no idea, when Susan opened her shop in Leesburg last year, that she'd had such a checkered past. "What happened?"

"Boating accident. Just the two of them. Boat sank, she survived, he didn't. He was the stronger swimmer and an experienced sailor. His body washed up on shore the day after the accident, and he had a cracked skull."

"Damn," Annie said, stunned at the revelation. "Well, isn't that interesting?"

"Yep," Gunnar said.

Annie was surprised. She and Susan hadn't talked much in their two encounters, but she'd seemed open and pleasant. "What did she say at the time?"

"Mike's getting the full deposition from the PD involved, but the news online says she said there was a problem with the rudder. He was bent over trying to fix it, a wave hit them, and he went overboard. The boat capsized, and she went in the water too. She never saw him come up and couldn't find him. But she's not a strong swimmer and admitted that she was afraid to get too far from the boat. Coast Guard found her clinging to it."

Annie shrugged. "That could have happened. He could have hit his head on the rudder when he went in the water."

"Sure. The cause of injury wasn't clear. Ultimately, they had to take her word for it because there was no proof that it didn't happen the way she said it did."

"And now she's being questioned in connection with another death by blow to the head. Do you believe in coincidences?" Annie asked.

"No," Gunnar answered grimly.

"Me either."

Annie felt a strange wave of relief. If Susan was their killer, she could be done with the whole mess and have a good outcome to report to her client. Laura would be pleased, and Annie would be a little richer. *All's well that ends well.* She found herself smiling and looking forward to the fund-raiser that evening.

"What are you so happy about?" Gunnar asked.

"I'm happy I don't have to handle all the paperwork for this case."

He snorted. "Nice."

Annie chuckled. "One of the perks of not being a cop anymore."

He glanced over at her. "But this has been kind of nice though, yeah? Like old times."

Annie smiled at him. "Yeah."

BY the time Annie had to get dressed for the Loudoun Chamber Music Association's Christmas fund-raiser, she was less enthusiastic about going than she had been previously. She was less sure of her new little black cocktail dress. It was about half an inch shorter than she was comfortable with, and the neckline plunged deeper than she remembered from the store. It had sequins and beading around the neck and at the bottom of the skirt, which had seemed elegant in the dressing-room mirror. In her bedroom, they seemed overdone.

By the time Celia arrived to pick her up, she was set not to go.

"Don't be ridiculous," Celia said. "You look fantastic. That dress is gorgeous. Come on, let's go." Annie was not convinced, but she pulled on her dress coat and followed Celia anyway.

The event was at Oatlands Plantation, one of Loudoun's oldest estates, just outside Leesburg on Route 15. The long driveway wound through an alley of trees, through which Annie could see the twinkling of candles in the windows of the yellow three-story mansion. Celia, no doubt in an effort to distract Annie from her unhappiness with the dress, carried on a one-sided conversation about the property, telling her the children of the last family to live there had donated the house and several hundred acres to the National Trust and that some of the other houses on the property were for rent and Annie should look into whether they were available and how much they rented for.

"I like my place in town," Annie insisted.

A parking attendant directed them toward the carriage house, a much smaller building where the fund-raiser was taking place. The carriage house was painted Williamsburg Blue. A wreath hung in every window, and another one adorned the lantern post outside the double front doors. For the first time all winter, Annie felt the Christmas spirit bubble up and was glad she'd agreed to come.

She and Celia checked their coats and were directed to the dining room, on the right. They found their table, and Annie looked around for the bar. She was surprised to see Laura Carlton standing at the head table, talking to two other women. As always, Laura was impeccably dressed, but no amount of makeup could cover how stressed she looked. That little bubble of Christmas cheer popped and drained right back out of Annie.

Laura looked up, and surprise registered on her face when she saw Annie. She excused herself from the conversation and walked over to where Annie and Celia were standing.

"I didn't know you liked chamber music," Laura said.

Annie thought of all the blues and rockabilly on her phone. She smiled. "Actually, I'm here as a guest." She turned to Celia. "This is my friend, Celia Armstrong."

Celia and Laura shook hands and exchanged greetings.

"Armstrong?" Laura said. "Are you—"

"Gary Armstrong's ex-wife, yes," Celia said.

"We all love Gary," Laura said then seemed to realize what she'd said.

Celia smiled graciously. "Gary's fantastic. I was so grateful that he offered me his tickets when he and Marc couldn't attend."

Laura smiled awkwardly. "That was sweet. They've been very supportive of our efforts the last few years."

"I'm sure. Marc especially loves chamber music," Celia said.

What she didn't say was that Gary didn't know a cello from an oboe, but he loved what Marc loved. Marc had been a music major in college and still played viola in a couple of music ensembles.

Another woman stopped and asked Laura a question about the appetizers.

Laura answered and then turned back to Celia and Annie. "I'm sorry. I'm chairman of the board for the Chamber Music Association. Nick and I ran this fund-raiser every year. To be honest, it's a bit overwhelming without him. He was so good with people." She smiled weakly. "I should get back to it. I hope you enjoy your evening."

Annie nodded. A string quartet began to play in the next room, and Annie and Celia each took a glass of white wine from a tray being circulated by a waiter.

Celia sighed as Laura walked away. "It's always so awkward to be the ex-wife of a gay guy."

"For what it's worth, you handle it well," Annie assured her.

"Thanks. I assume that's the same Laura Carlton that hired you?" Celia asked.

"The one and only."

Celia took a sip of wine. "Crazy. She looks pretty strung out. Nice dress, though."

"Frankly," Annie said, "I'm surprised she can function at all."

"I don't know," Celia said. "Maybe she needed to get out of the house, and this provided a distraction."

Annie nodded. "I can see her as the type that would want to work to deal with the grief."

"I know I would," Celia said.

The room filled up until the carriage house seemed to be at capacity. A couple that Celia knew came over and talked to them, and Annie snacked happily on any hors d'oeuvres that floated by on waiters' trays. The entire event was very elegant. The men were all in tuxedos, and the women were in glittering beaded and sequined cocktail dresses, which made Annie feel better about her own choice of dress. All the tables had crisp gold tablecloths and centerpieces of evergreen boughs wrapped around red and green candles. The atmosphere was very festive, and the chamber music was better than Annie had expected it to be. She didn't know most of the songs, but she recognized a few Christmas favorites like "What Child Is This?" and "Silent Night."

Annie noticed Eddie Peabody in the other room as she and Celia circulated among the silent-auction items. Annie wrote her bids down for a basket full of dog toys and for a numbered print by local artist Kate Abernethy. Annie had seen the print in some of the galleries in Leesburg and really liked it but couldn't afford to buy one. She probably wouldn't win the silent auction either, but she gave it a try. Celia had high hopes for winning either a horse-themed basket or a knitting-themed basket. Annie had fun wandering around, drinking wine and keeping a hopeful eye on the auctions. Annie was really glad Celia had invited her. They kept running into people Annie recognized. Doctors, judges, and county board members seemed to be everywhere.

Laura Carlton seemed to be everywhere as well, and Annie noticed that people seemed to be eyeing her a lot with whispers and furtive glances. Being suspected of her husband's murder must have been awful. Annie caught a snippet of conversation between two women.

The older of the two said, "I think Laura should step down from the board in light of the scandal."

The younger woman frowned and said, "Oh please. You just want her seat."

The older woman stormed off in a huff. Annie wondered how many similar conversations were going on in the room. A general tension was definitely rippling through the crowd. While being here couldn't have been easy for Laura, she seemed to be handling it well. When David Cohen showed up, Laura was visibly more relaxed, as if she felt she needed her lawyer to even get through a social engagement.

Eddie was also more and more visible as the evening went on. He stopped to speak to several people and seemed to be making the rounds as much as Laura was, as if he was also a host. Annie wondered if he'd stepped in to take Nick's place or if he regularly cohosted the event. She felt bad for him. The guy was awkward and seemed out of his depth, but he was certainly trying.

At eight o'clock, Laura stood at a podium surrounded by poinsettias and called everyone to dinner. She introduced the speaker, who was the director or the conductor of the Chamber Music Association. Annie wasn't sure which term was correct or if the two were interchangeable. She was just happy he didn't speak for too long since she understood little of what he was talking about.

Dinner was standard event fare: lemon chicken, rice pilaf, and mixed vegetables, with coffee and chocolate cake for dessert. It wasn't the best meal she'd ever had, but the chicken wasn't too rubbery, and it beat eating alone. She and Celia chatted with the people at their table and discovered they knew some of the same people in the sheriff's office.

After dinner came dancing. A tall handsome man asked Celia to dance. She accepted, but as he led her out onto the dance floor, Celia glanced back at Annie with a brief expression of panic. Annie smiled at her and waved her on. Celia hadn't been on a date for a long time, and Annie felt a little dancing might be good for her. The tall handsome guy turned out to be a good dancer and kept Celia on the dance floor for over an hour. Annie drank another glass of wine as she enjoyed the light catching the sequins on the women's dresses as the couples moved to the music. She noticed Eddie dancing with Laura until David Cohen asked to cut in. Eddie shot a dirty look at the attorney as Cohen danced away with Laura. At eleven o'clock, the quartet ended its set, and Laura began announcing the winners of the silent auction. Celia sat back down next to Annie, practically glowing.

Annie smiled at her. "Make a new friend?"

"That," said Celia, "was Ted Whitt. He owns a vineyard a few miles west of me."

"Oh, does he?" Annie said, raising her eyebrows.

Celia blushed. "Stop it. I want to hear if we won anything."

Annie laughed. "Sure you do."

As expected, they didn't win anything, and as the event wound down, they made their way out with the rest of the crowd. Annie noticed Laura and Eddie standing with David Cohen and thanking everyone and saying their goodbyes by the door. They all looked exhausted.

By the time Celia dropped her off, midnight was approaching, and Annie was too sleepy from the wine to think about anything but going to bed.

CHAPTER SEVENTEEN
Friday

A t eight o'clock the following morning, Annie's cell phone woke her from her deep, wine-soaked sleep. "What?" she croaked into the phone.

"Jenny Tomlin fell down the stairs of her apartment building last night," Gunnar said.

Annie sat up in bed. "What?"

"Jenny Tomlin—"

"I heard you," Annie said, wiping the sleep from her eyes. "Is she okay?"

"No. She's unconscious in Fairfax Hospital."

"Jesus," Annie said, getting out of bed. "What happened?"

"It's unclear whether she fell or was pushed, but a neighbor thought he heard arguing upstairs but wasn't sure which floor or if Jenny was one of the people involved."

"What the hell?" Annie said.

Gunnar sighed. "I know. What's the point of going after her?"

"It has to be about the baby, right?" Annie said.

"Then we're back to the wife."

"If this happened last night, then it definitely wasn't Laura."

"Annie," Gunnar said, his voice stern and disapproving.

"Seriously, Gun, I was with Laura most of last night."

"What?" Gunnar said. "You're her alibi?"

"No," Annie said reflexively. "I mean, yes, I guess, but me and, like, a hundred other people."

"What? Look, do you mind if we don't do this over the phone? I'm on my way into the station. Can I just stop by for a couple of minutes?"

"Sure," Annie said as she pulled on a pair of jeans.

WITH Gunnar on his way over, Annie looked around at her apartment and realized what a mess it was. Clothes were strewn all over the floor and sofa where she'd dropped everything the night before. She started a pot of coffee and ran a brush through her hair before scooping up all the clothes and throwing them on her bed. Gunnar got there just as the coffee maker finished gurgling.

"Hey, that was quick," Annie said when she opened the door.

Gunnar looked tired. "Thanks for seeing me."

"It's not a problem," she said, handing him a cup of coffee.

"Thanks. I really need this," he said as he settled on the sofa.

Annie kept an eye on Gunnar while she poured herself some coffee. He looked as though he hadn't been sleeping, and his face was red. She worried about his blood pressure and regretted offering him coffee.

"You doing okay?" she asked. "You look pretty beat."

He rubbed a huge hand down his face and then over his head, leaving his thick blond hair pointing out in all directions. "I am beat. When my buddy Paul at Fairfax PD called me about Jenny Tomlin this morning, I about lost it. What the hell is going on with this case?"

"So there's no chance she just fell?" Annie asked.

"They're not sure, but Fairfax PD is treating it as suspicious. A downstairs neighbor heard a man and a woman arguing in the stairwell on one of the floors above him, but he wasn't sure who they were, and he couldn't make out exactly what was being said. Then he heard Jenny scream. When he went to investigate, he found Jenny unconscious at the bottom of the stairs and no one else around."

"That doesn't sound like an accident."

"No," Gunnar said. "She's at Fairfax Hospital in the ICU. So far, the baby is okay, but I get the feeling that's kind of touch and go."

Annie sighed and sat down on the other end of the sofa. She felt sick. "Does Fairfax have any leads?"

"No, except Paul knew she was interviewed in conjunction with our case."

"What about security cameras?" Annie asked. "I saw a couple when I was there."

"None of them are working. The building manager said the system has been down for two weeks and that they're planning to upgrade the whole thing."

"Sure they are. I'd be surprised if they were ever even connected to a system," Annie said. "And I bet she pays extra for the cameras and the security door."

Gunnar frowned. "Yeah, for all the good it did her."

"What time of day did it happen?"

"The neighbor said it was around seven p.m." He took a sip of his coffee and closed his eyes appreciatively.

"And no one saw anything?" Annie sighed.

That was a bad time of day for witnesses. People were either home from work and in for the night or they'd already gone out.

"No. She has three neighbors on her floor, and only one was home, but she was in the shower and had the TV on, so she didn't hear anything. No one saw anyone suspicious leaving the building. A woman who lives on the first floor said she saw a guy leaving the building around that time, but she couldn't describe him beyond she thought he was white and might've had brown hair. He was wearing a red baseball cap, but she didn't remember any kind of logo on it. She was opening her door, and her kid was screaming, so she wasn't exactly giving the guy in the hat her full attention. She didn't hear Tomlin scream, and she didn't think she could pick the guy out of a lineup."

Annie leaned her head back against the sofa. "Do they think that was even the same guy?"

"It could be. She said her kid was screaming when they got out of the car because he wanted to go to McDonald's or something, and her apartment is the first one inside the door, so theoretically, that guy could have pushed her down the stairs. She fell from the fourth-floor landing to the third-floor landing, and then he could have walked down the rest of the stairs and passed by the woman and her kid. But it doesn't matter anyway since no one can identify him."

"So that doesn't rule out Susan," Annie said thoughtfully.

"No. We don't know that was the guy that threw Tomlin down the stairs. We don't even know for sure it was a man. It could have been Susan. She's a tall woman, and she's no soprano. The neighbor could have mistaken her voice for a man's."

"Did Susan even know about Jenny?"

Gunnar shrugged. "I don't know." He looked at his watch. "I intend to find out when I meet with her and her lawyer at nine o'clock."

"Well, at least we know it wasn't Laura," Annie said.

Gunnar raised his eyebrows. "Yeah, how's that exactly?"

"The time frame rules her out. She's chairman of the board for the Loudoun County Chamber Music Association, and last night was their Christmas fund-raiser at Oatlands. I got there just after seven o'clock, and she was already there. I suspect she had been there for a while setting up too. Even if she took the toll road and was speeding through a magic traffic window leaving Arlington, it would've taken at least forty-five minutes. Not to mention Laura's not exactly scrappy, and she *is* a soprano."

Gunnar smiled and scratched at the stubble on his cheek. "True. I'll have someone check exactly when she arrived, though. Wouldn't want to be accused of not being thorough."

Annie felt bad for him. The newspaper article had to have hurt him.

"I'm sure there were several people setting up the carriage house who can vouch for her," she said.

"How about Susan? Was she there?"

"Not that I saw. Eddie Peabody was there." Annie finished her coffee. Gunnar had already drained his.

"The whole time?"

"The first time I saw him was before dinner at eight o'clock. I don't know if he was there before that. The dinner was divided between the two rooms of the carriage house, so I couldn't see everyone. Susan could have been there, and I might not have seen her, but during the course of the night, I probably would have. She's kind of hard to miss."

Gunnar tugged at his bottom lip. "Great, so now I've probably got to interview all those people to see who was where when."

Annie refilled their cups.

"All these interviews are killing me. It feels like a huge waste of resources. None of the women Nick slept with from that website even knew him well enough to want to kill him, and the husbands we're finding are either just as kinky as their wives or they didn't know about the website. Fairfax PD is running prints in the apartment stairwell and on Jenny Tomlin's door to see if any of them match the prints on Nick's phone, to try and make a connection. Is it wrong that I'm hoping to God they find Susan's prints? I just want to put this damn case to bed."

Annie sighed. "It's not wrong, but you know they're bound to find hundreds of prints in that stairwell. It'll take forever to process them all."

"I know, but they're a big department with plenty of money. They can afford the time and manpower to do it."

"True." Annie nodded. "But her prints weren't on the phone."

Gunnar shrugged. "Maybe they were and they just aren't in our system. We've inquired with the St. Lucia Police Department to see if they fingerprinted her. If so, they'll send us a set, and we'll find out if her prints are some of the ones that haven't been identified from the phone."

"Maybe you'll get lucky, and Susan will just confess during the meeting. Wouldn't that be great?"

Gunnar smiled. "Yeah, that would be great."

Annie stood and took his empty coffee cup. "Of course, the two cases could be unrelated."

Gunnar looked up at her. "Do they seem unrelated to you?"

"No. But I don't understand why Susan would throw Jenny Tomlin down the stairs."

Gunnar sighed. "Aside from Laura, who might have done it out of jealousy, it doesn't make sense that anyone would do that. I mean, who even knew about Jenny Tomlin?"

Annie put the coffee cups in the sink and rubbed her temples. She had a headache from too much wine the night before. "I don't know, but I don't see how Laura could have done it, and I'm not sure Eddie could have either. So if it wasn't Laura and it wasn't Eddie, that leaves Susan."

"And the seventy-nine women and their boyfriends and husbands that we haven't interviewed yet."

"But why would any of them have attacked Jenny Tomlin?"

"I have no idea." He blew out a frustrated breath.

Annie sat next to him on the sofa. "You know, it actually crossed my mind that maybe Laura and Eddie worked this out together at the Chamber Music Association meetings, but I'm fairly certain that's crazy."

Gunnar smiled at her. "If we were living in some cozy English village and Nick had been clubbed on the head with a violin instead of a rock, you might have something."

Annie smiled at him. "It's good to see you haven't lost your sense of humor."

He looked at her with a serious expression. "You're sure it's not possible, though?"

"I don't think so. They only meet once a month, and Nick was on the board too. Besides, what's the motive? Eddie and Laura don't appear to be having an affair. Why else would they do something like that?"

He sighed. "I hope to God Fairfax PD finds some decent clues in their case because they don't seem to exist in mine."

They sat in silence for a moment.

Gunnar looked askance at her. "Since when do you listen to chamber music?"

"Since Celia offered me a free ticket to dinner and an open wine bar."

He chuckled. "Understood."

Annie looked at him. He really did look bad.

"So how are things going with you?" she asked. "Aside from the case. Everything okay?"

He looked her in the eye before staring at the floor. "Honestly, not so hot. Diane and I are in marriage counseling. I'm sleeping in the guest room. What that newspaper article implied about you and me didn't help."

"Sullivan's a jerk." Annie didn't know Diane well, but Gunnar had always seemed rock-solid about his marriage. "I'm sorry you guys are having problems."

"Diane is having problems. I thought things were fine, but then, what do I know?"

Annie wasn't sure what he meant by that. "So is it helping?"

"The counseling? I don't know. I don't think so. I think she was done before she suggested it. She's probably only going so she can say she tried everything. I can't believe this is happening again."

Annie knew he'd been married for a couple of years right out of college.

He shook his head. "You know, I thought the first time it was because we were too young, but now... maybe it's just me."

"It's not you. It's the job."

"Thanks, but other cops manage to stay married."

"But a lot of them don't," Annie insisted.

Gunnar leaned forward, resting his elbows on his knees. He laced his fingers together and stared at the floor again. "I don't know. Blaming the job seems like a lame excuse."

She nudged him with her shoulder. "I'm glad you were never as hard on me as you are on yourself. I don't think I could've taken it."

He chuckled again, but the sound had turned sad. "I don't know. It's all coming down around my ears. Can't fix my marriage. Can't solve this case."

"We'll solve the case. It's clearly escalating. Whoever is behind this is bound to slip up soon."

Gunnar snorted. "Well, I wish they'd hurry up."

"Maybe Fairfax PD will turn up something at the apartment."

"Great." Gunnar frowned. "Then the Great State of Fairfax gets to be the hero because the little town of Leesburg can't solve its own problems."

Annie sighed. "Don't be like that. You said it yourself. They've got the money and the manpower."

Gunnar shook his head. "I'm so tired of being on the short end of the stick."

"You'll get him. I have faith."

He looked at her and gave her a half smile. "Then you're the only one."

Annie sat back against the sofa cushions and tried to think about the case in a different way. "Don't you think it's weird that a lot of these people went to high school together?"

Gunnar shrugged. "Not really. Back when they were in school, there were only eighty-some thousand people in the whole county. Leesburg was a lot smaller then."

"Yeah, I know," Annie said. "But people move on, move away. How many people do you see on a regular basis that you went to high school with?"

He considered the question. "I don't know. A couple. Kurt Davis, who works over in land records—I see him sometimes in the county building. And another guy I went to school with manages the Ford service center, and I usually see him when I take the car in. That's about it."

"Right," Annie nodded. "I see exactly zero people I went to high school with on a regular basis. Every once in a while, I run into someone during the Christmas holidays when I'm in Arlington shopping or something. But other than that, almost never."

"Okay," Gunnar said. "What's your point?"

"I don't know, just that these are people with deep roots. Maybe this is more complicated than just sex or money."

Gunnar chuckled. "Okay, Sherlock. What's the big conspiracy?"

She rolled her eyes at him. "I'm not saying there's some big hidden agenda. I'm just saying maybe there's something that we're missing."

"Well, obviously we're missing something. We haven't solved it."

"Yeah, I know. But do you see what I'm saying?"

Gunnar shook his head. "No. These people are too long out of school for that to matter. Not to mention we're talking about really well-educated people here. They all went to college and have good jobs. They aren't exactly a bunch of losers sitting around with nothing to do but think about old wrongs from twenty years ago."

Annie closed her eyes and pinched the bridge of her nose to try to relieve the headache. "You might be right."

"Of course I'm right," Gunnar said, standing and stretching. "Nick Carlton was killed over sex. You live by the sword, you die by it."

"Okay, then who killed him?"

"I don't know yet, but I've got a lot more suspects to interview."

"Well, I'm going to poke around a bit in his past."

"Go right ahead," Gunnar said. "It can't hurt. I've got to go."

WHEN Gunnar left, Annie finished the employee background checks she'd been doing for the local telecommunications company. She emailed the report at three o'clock and decided to go ahead and get dressed for dinner at her father's house and head east for the rest of the day. Before she left her apartment, she pulled out a clear vase Ford had sent her flowers in ages ago and took it with her.

"Come on, little man," she called to Chester, and the two of them went out to the car.

Annie wanted to stop at Fairfax Hospital and check on Jenny Tomlin before she went to her father's. She remembered that Jenny's family was in California, and she didn't like to think of the poor woman lying there alone.

A Giant grocery store was near the hospital, and Annie popped in to buy flowers for the vase. She preferred not to pay hospital-gift-shop prices, but she still wanted to take some flowers. That way, if Jenny woke up, she would see someone had been there.

Annie left Chester in the car in the hospital parking lot, knowing the temperature was cold enough that he would be okay. The woman at the information desk in the main building directed her to the intensive care unit. Annie walked through the long white corridors to the right bank of elevators. Fairfax Hospital was more heavily populated than some small towns, and the massive complex had several buildings and could be difficult to navigate. An effort had been made to liven the place up with public art and photos of staff, but being back here still gave Annie the creeps. Fairfax had a level-one trauma unit, and Annie had been flown here after she was shot. She didn't remember any of that, but she did remember some of her time in neuro ICU and then on the regular neuro floor. Thinking about it left her feeling vaguely nauseated. She rubbed at the scar on the side of her head and was happy when the elevator doors opened. She was starting to feel claustrophobic.

Unlike the lobby, the intensive care unit had that distinct hospital smell. Annie had to force herself off the elevator. The nurse in ICU told her their patients couldn't have flowers in their rooms. Annie kicked herself for forgetting that detail from her own stay. She left the flowers at the nurses' station and looked in on Jenny.

She was unconscious, very small and pale in the hospital bed, and hooked to all manner of monitoring equipment. Her right arm was in a cast, and the right side of her face was badly bruised. Annie backed out of the room and turned back to the nurses' station. The low beeps and occasional hiss of equipment followed her, and she felt closed in. Her palms were starting to sweat.

Be a big girl, she thought, trying to force herself to calm down. "Has there been any change?" Annie asked a nurse at the duty station.

"Not yet," the nurse said, "but that doesn't mean there won't be. She could still come out of this."

Annie nodded. "Has her family been called? They're in California."

"Yes. I believe they're flying in tonight."

"Good." She started to tremble. She needed to get out of there.

"You're a friend?"

"We know each other through work," Annie said quickly, trying to tune out the noises and ignore the smell.

"You just missed one of her other coworkers," the nurse told her.

Annie was happy Jenny Tomlin hadn't spent the day alone, but then she had a disturbing thought. "Did the other person leave their name?"

"No," the nurse said. "She just left those flowers on the desk and took a quick peek at Miss Tomlin and left."

"Oh," Annie said. "Are those the flowers there?"

The nurse nodded and went to check on a patient.

Annie took a deep, calming breath and checked the flowers for a card. It was a business card. On the back was written "We all miss you. Get well soon." She flipped it over. The card was from Nina Mako at Potomac Telecomm. Annie took a photo of the card with her cell phone. Doing that took three tries because her hands were shaking. The information probably wouldn't amount to anything, but she wanted to give it to Gunnar anyway.

She hurried to the elevator and blinked back panicky tears as it descended. She had to force herself not to run through the lobby, but once she hit the parking lot, she did run the short distance to her car as fast as she could, which wasn't very. Pain shot up her leg every time her right foot hit the pavement, but she kept running.

She hadn't anticipated reacting like that to being at the hospital. She'd never been prone to panic, but she wasn't sure how else to describe what she'd felt standing in the ICU. No matter how absurd, she couldn't shake the feeling that she would somehow be trapped there, disoriented and hooked to a million machines. She was trembling, and despite the fact that the temperature was just above freezing outside, she was sweating by the time she reached the car. She let Chester out of his crate, and he licked her face. She sat with him in her lap for a while until her heart rate slowed back to normal.

CHAPTER EIGHTEEN
Friday Night

The last thing she wanted to do now was go to her father's house for dinner with her aunts, but she put the car in gear and headed to Arlington anyway. Irrational panic wasn't going to send her scurrying back home.

Her Aunt Peggy's blue Buick was in the driveway when Annie pulled in. Her great-aunt Ginny no longer drove and lived with Peggy, so they were both probably there. Annie sighed. She put Chester on his leash, opened the gate, and took him through the side yard to the back of the house. Joey was painting in the sunroom. Even when it was cold, he liked to paint in there, so he was wearing a winter jacket, the one he called his painting coat, which had streaks of color all over it. Annie tapped lightly on the door to catch his attention. He gave her a broad grin when he saw her. She put her finger to her lips to make sure he didn't announce her arrival and then motioned for him to come outside.

Joey slipped out the door and closed it softly behind him. He loved the "sneaky-quiet game," which they'd been playing since they were kids. Joey gave Annie a big hug and picked up Chester, who proceeded to lick his chin.

"No licking," Annie said reflexively, but she knew it was pointless. Joey never minded Chester's kisses, and Chester loved giving them.

"So the aunts are here?" Annie said.

"Yes," Joey said.

She looked at her watch. "Cocktails already started?"

"Yes," Joey said.

"Great." She sat down on a bench on the patio, and Joey sat next to her. "I've had kind of a crap day."

Joey nodded. "Me too."

"Yeah?" Annie asked. "What happened to you?"

Her brother didn't usually say things like that.

"My girlfriend's mother said she can't be my girlfriend anymore."

Annie raised her eyebrows and smiled. This was unexpected. "I didn't know you had a girlfriend, buddy."

Joey let out a big sigh. "Yeah, we met at the recycling center. Her name is Mary, and she's really nice."

"So what happened with her mother?"

His face fell. "Her mother doesn't think she should have a boyfriend."

"Oh." Annie felt terrible for him.

"It's not fair," Joey said, tears welling in his brown eyes.

Annie put her arm around him. "I know, buddy."

"I really like Mary, and she really likes me. I'm a man, and I have a job, and I should have a girlfriend too."

"How about Mary? How old is she?" Joey didn't always recognize age differences, and Annie wondered if that was the reason for Mary's mother's reluctance.

Joey wiped his eyes on his jacket sleeve. "Only a year younger than me. That's old enough to have a boyfriend," he said with conviction.

Annie nodded. "I think so."

A cold breeze blew through the yard, rustling the leaves against the tall wooden privacy fence.

Annie shivered. "We should probably go in. It's cold out here."

"Yeah," Joey said.

"I'm sorry about your girlfriend. Maybe her mom will change her mind."

"Maybe." That thought seemed to lift his spirits as they went inside.

The moment they stepped into the sunroom, they could hear the conversation from the living room. Aunt Ginny was going deaf but refused to wear a hearing aid, so evenings with her resulted in a lot of shouting. Tonight's topic seemed to be hockey. Ginny was a huge sports fan and very devoted to local teams. She had season tickets to the Capitals, the Redskins, the Nationals, and even DC United. She'd once owned her own decorating firm and had done quite well with business accounts all over DC and the Virginia and Maryland suburbs of the city, but she'd sold the business and retired a few years before. These days, she devoted herself to sports fandom. The house where she and Peggy lived was filled with memorabilia.

When Annie and Joey came into the living room, Aunt Ginny was sitting in one corner of the sofa, pounding her small fist on the end table. "And that's why they've got to get him off the roster."

On the opposite side of the room, Aunt Peggy was sitting in a wingback chair, staring out the window and sipping her scotch and soda. Annie's father was in the other wingback, nursing a bourbon and Coke.

"If only you were the coach," he said dryly.

"Damn straight!" Ginny declared and took a fierce drink of her Manhattan, eyes blazing.

Her father caught sight of her in the doorway. "Annie!" He got up to give her a hug.

Joey set Chester down, and the little dog immediately jumped on the sofa and into Ginny's lap. She patted him on the head and cooed at him.

"Ah," her father muttered. "Chester soothes the savage beast."

Annie chuckled.

"Gin and tonic?"

"Please."

Her father stepped to the bar cart in the corner of the room to mix her drink.

Peggy came over and hugged her, and Annie leaned down and kissed her aunt Ginny on the cheek.

Her father handed her the cocktail. "Dinner should be ready in a few minutes."

"Do you need any help?" Annie asked.

"Nope. Relax and enjoy your drink. I'm just going to finish up."

Annie settled on the sofa, and Joey took the wingback chair their father had abandoned. Aunt Ginny started on hockey again, so Annie let her mind wander. She liked hockey, but she didn't follow it seriously enough to understand most of what her aunt was going on about.

She thought about her father cooking and tried to remember whether he had ever cooked before her mother died. She couldn't remember—maybe he had grilled some. She did, however, remember the disastrous results of some of his early attempts at making a meal. Being a smart man, successful in his field, her father seemed to think that he should be able to walk into the kitchen and whip up whatever he wanted without much difficulty. The problem was that what he wanted wasn't simple fare. After several failed attempts, he set about studying cooking as if he were planning on opening his own restaurant. Over time, he got the results he wanted, and now dinner at the Fitches' was an invitation few turned down. Once a month, though, Friday dinner was reserved for family, which meant just the four of them. Ford was welcome, too, when he was in town, but generally he found somewhere else to be. Annie would have preferred if the guest list was more open, but she suspected her father closed it more to protect his friends from Ginny's sports rants than out of any great and abiding respect for family unity.

Aunt Peggy was staring out the window again, and Joey was trying to get Chester to leave Ginny's lap and come to him. Chester loved Ginny, and she adored him right back. Unfortunately, her adoration didn't change her focus—she continued her tirade about the Capitals lineup and who should be traded and who should stay, which segued as it always did into who were the best players she'd ever seen—and she'd seen plenty. Annie was never so grateful as when her father called everyone to the table. At least Ginny was too polite to speak with her mouth full.

Her father had outdone himself. Dinner was a beef-rib roast with mashed potatoes and gravy, creamed onions, roasted Brussels sprouts, and Yorkshire pudding.

Joey grinned broadly and rubbed his hands together. "Yum!"

"Have a seat," her father said. He poured everyone but Joey a glass of red wine and gave Joey a glass of beer.

Annie smiled. Joey didn't like the taste of wine, but he did enjoy the occasional beer, and her father didn't fuss about it. He always felt strongly that Joey should feel as normal for a man his age as possible, and if he wanted a beer, that was just fine.

"To family and winter feasts," her father said and held his glass up for a toast.

Everyone clinked glasses and passed their plates up as her father carved the roast. Aside from the minor comments needed to pass dishes around, the table was blissfully quiet while everyone ate.

"Where's Ford tonight?" her aunt Peggy eventually asked.

"Working," Annie said and hoped the conversation about Ford would end there.

Of course, it didn't.

"He works so much," Peggy commented.

"He has one of those jobs," Annie said, once again hoping to end the conversation. She was too tired to have the whole conversation about him being back overseas. She wished Ginny would just go back to her hockey rant.

"When are you two going to get married?" Ginny demanded, smacking her hand against the table.

Something inside Annie clicked, and before she could stop it, a wave of frustration and exhaustion welled up and roared out. "How about never!"

All movement at the table ceased.

"Excuse me," Annie said through clenched teeth. She dropped her napkin on the table and stormed out.

SHE wanted to drive home, but her father had poured her a strong gin and tonic, and she'd already finished most of her glass of wine at dinner. Frustrated, she went upstairs to her old bedroom. Chester, sensing Annie's distress, followed her. Annie closed the bedroom door behind him and plopped down on an old pink IKEA club chair in the corner of the room. Chester jumped onto her lap.

"You're a good boy," she told him.

She leaned her head back against the chair and took a deep breath. She shouldn't have yelled at Ginny. Now the whole family would be discussing her and Ford. They were probably down there whispering about it. Inevitably, she was going to have talk to her father about it, which was a conversation she really didn't want to have.

"Why am I so stupid, Chester?"

Chester licked her chin.

Annie sighed. "Yeah. I don't know either."

Losing her temper like that wasn't normal for her. She looked around at the bedroom. She'd stayed here when she was recovering from the shooting, but little evidence of the adult her remained. Everything from the softball trophies and science-fair ribbon to posters from the bands she'd liked in high school were largely untouched. Her father's maid kept everything dusted, giving it the effect of a shrine to her seventeen-year-old self.

A picture of her and Ford, taken poolside at a party at the end of senior year, sat on the desk. He was behind her with his arms around her, and they were both tan and smiling. For some reason, that was how she always thought of him, tan and happy in the sunshine, but when she really considered it, he hadn't been that guy in a long time. For that matter, she wasn't that girl anymore either.

That was an odd thing about traumatic brain injury. She'd spent the whole recovery period desperate to feel like herself. Eventually, she got to a point where she felt so much better that she started to feel that maybe she was her old self. Not until later did she realize she wasn't. She was more emotional and less focused but also less uptight and less anxious. Before, she'd constantly analyzed the past, looking for things to avoid in the future. Now, she mostly lived in the moment, the past and the future slipping around her unanalyzed. Once, she had been very driven about being a police officer. She'd pushed herself hard to make detective and was the youngest woman, and among the youngest people, ever to do so in Leesburg PD. At one time, she'd dreamed about being a captain or maybe even chief of the whole department. Somehow, when she'd woken from her coma, all that drive and ambition had slipped away.

When she had been on the force, she hated every minute of doing stakeouts. Now, she liked the waiting and watching. She felt patient and connected to the world around her in ways she never had before. She sighed. Maybe that was her problem—she'd recovered as a stranger. In the back of her mind, she wondered if that was why Ford had decided to take overseas assignments again. Maybe this new version of her wasn't who he wanted to be with, and he had just realized he was never going to get the old her back.

A light knock came at the door. It opened a crack, and her father said, "Annie?"

"Come in, Dad."

"How's it going, kiddo?"

He sat down on the edge of the bed, facing her. He had two cocktails with him and handed her the gin and tonic. She considered whether or not to drink it, but since she'd already had too much to drive, she figured drinking more didn't matter.

Annie took a sip and sighed. "I'm really sorry."

Her father shrugged. "We've all snapped at Ginny at one time or another. She can be irritating. It happens. Peggy's taking her home now."

"I should go apologize."

"Don't. She'll get over it. She knows she's annoying. I'm more concerned about what's going on with you."

Annie closed her eyes and tried to swallow the lump that had formed in her throat. Her father waited patiently, sipping his bourbon.

"I don't know," Annie said in a hoarse whisper. "Maybe it's nothing."

"What kind of nothing?"

Annie looked up at him. She hadn't expected him to probe for more answers. "Ford went back overseas."

Her father nodded. "Okay. And?"

"And nothing. He's taken some foreign assignments lately. He really hasn't done that for the last year, and I don't know what that means. I thought things had changed with us. That he wanted to make things more... I don't know... I think I might have misinterpreted what he wanted out of our relationship."

Her father looked puzzled. "I don't understand. Did he say something to suggest... Did you two have an argument?"

"No. I'm probably just being stupid. Don't worry about it, okay?"

Her father sipped his drink and seemed to contemplate what she'd said. "Maybe you don't realize this, Annie, but Ford and I spent a tremendous amount of time together after you were shot."

Annie looked at him, not sure where he was going.

"He loves you. I don't know what happened with you two recently, but I know he loves you."

Annie couldn't stop the tears from falling. "I just don't think he wants this."

"What are you talking about? He bathed you. He fed you. He took extended leave from work to be here for your recovery. I don't know how I would have managed without him."

Annie pushed the tears off her cheeks. "You think I don't know that? He's a good man, and I know he loves me, but come on, Dad." She pressed her fingertips against the long scar, which had started to ache.

"What?"

She shook her head, tears slipping down her cheeks. "I'm not the same."

Her father leaned over and put a hand on her knee. "No one expects you to be. All of us are changed by events in our lives. I'm not the same man I was when your mother was alive. Some of that is because she died, and some of it is because I'm a lot older now. But I'm certainly not the same."

Annie smiled at him through her tears. "But if you met someone now, they wouldn't know who you were before. Ford is still here, and I'm not the same."

Her father sighed and sat back. "I'm not sure you're giving him very much credit. And you're kind of selling him short on his own changes. It seems to me he came back from Afghanistan changed by the experience. You're telling me you didn't notice that?"

Annie closed her eyes. "Of course I did."

"And you still love him despite the changes."

"Yes."

"So if you can love him through his changes, why can't he love you through yours?"

She considered that. "I don't know."

"I think you're upset that he's so far away, and you're making more of it than there really is."

Annie shrugged. "Maybe. Do you mind if I stay here tonight? I've had too much to drink to drive home."

"You can always stay here, Annie. You don't have to ask."

Annie smiled at him. "Thanks, Dad."

STAYING overnight at her father's house turned out to be a terrible idea. Every time she dozed off, she woke up panicked, as if she were still recovering from the shooting. She knew the dreams were precipitated by the conversation with her father and seeing Jenny Tomlin in the hospital, but the feeling of being vulnerable, as though she would never get better, was hard to shake. When she couldn't stand it anymore, she got up and went downstairs. The house was quiet. She found herself walking in circles: living room, kitchen, dining room, parlor, over and over. She'd done the same thing when she first got out of the hospital. Her sleep schedule had been off, so she would wake at odd hours and walk through the house to remind her brain that it could move all the muscles in her legs, to explain to her body that it didn't need to drag her right foot. Doing the loop through the house was much easier now. Chester followed her, confused about what they were doing and why they were doing it so early. Loyal to a fault, the little terrier kept to her heels.

Annie noticed all the changes as she walked. Her father had bought a new, larger flat-screen TV for the living room. A new lamp was in the living room, and someone had replaced the kitchen curtains. Annie suspected her aunt Peggy because she couldn't imagine her father even noticing the kitchen had curtains. She continued to circle through the house, trying to tire herself out enough to go back to sleep.

Something in the circling was comforting. The ease with which she made the trek reminded that her she was better, that the nightmares were just that and not some sign that she was slipping. After a few more laps through the house, she found a book on ancient Egypt in the parlor and settled down to read until everyone else was up. She considered just going home, but Joey would be really disappointed if she left without saying goodbye. He had been quite excited the night before when he found out she was staying.

CHAPTER NINETEEN
Saturday

H er father was up at six, turning off the outside lights and opening the blinds. He was startled to find her in the living room.

"Hey, kiddo, what are you doing up so early?"

Annie shrugged. "Oh, you know."

He father stopped opening the blinds and looked at her. "You look beat."

"I haven't been sleeping much lately. There's a lot on my mind."

"You know you shouldn't let yourself get too tired. The doctor said—"

Chester started his let's-go-out dance, and Annie excused herself to take him. She didn't think she was up for another conversation with her father, particularly one about her health. He hovered and fussed over her too much.

When she and Chester returned from the backyard, the smell of bacon was wafting through the house. Joey was up and sitting at the kitchen bar, watching their father cook.

"How does bacon and waffles sound?" her father asked.

"I think it sounds great," Joey said enthusiastically, bouncing on his barstool.

Annie slid onto the stool next to his. She wished she could muster half of his enthusiasm for any little thing. "Me too."

Her father had music playing. "The Weight" by the Band came on. Joey grinned and sang along, singing louder whenever Annie's name was mentioned. Annie laughed because the woman in the song was named Fanny, but this was lost on Joey. The song had been her mother's favorite, and he had been singing it wrong for years.

Breakfast was delicious, and the conversation was blissfully benign. Her father talked about cleaning out the garage since it was supposed to be a nice day. Joey said he could help after work. Annie didn't say much. She just enjoyed her breakfast and hoped the rest of the day would be that easy.

IT wasn't. When her father and brother left for the recycling center at nine o'clock, Annie left for Leesburg. On the way home, Laura Carlton called. She wanted Annie to meet her and her lawyer at her home at eleven. Annie agreed and took Chester back to the apartment, where she showered and changed into a work outfit. She assumed Laura would want an update on the case, but Annie couldn't tell her much. Gunnar hadn't called yet about the interview with Susan, so she had nothing new to tell Laura.

At the end of Royal Street, Annie pulled into the small lot next to King Street Coffee, where she managed to snag the last available parking space. A group of moms and their toddlers just beat her to the counter, so by the time she got her large coffee to go, Annie was a few minutes late getting to Laura's house. When she arrived, Laura ushered her into the kitchen, where David Cohen sat at the table with no tie on and the top two buttons of his dress shirt undone. He looked incredibly comfortable sitting at Laura's kitchen table, and Laura looked better than she had since the whole thing started. She had some color back in her cheeks, and she looked slim instead of gaunt.

Interesting, Annie thought. Laura certainly wouldn't be the first woman to fall for her lawyer. That put David Cohen in a whole new category in Annie's mind. She wondered how long the affair been going on and whether that meant adding Cohen to the suspect list. She tried to remember if she'd seen any inkling of romance the first time she'd seen them together.

"I was just making some sandwiches," Laura said. "Would you like one?"

"Sure," Annie said, still sizing up the two of them.

"Chicken salad or ham and cheese?"

"Ham and cheese sounds good."

"David, could you get everyone a glass of tea?" Laura asked as she opened deli containers and started the sandwiches.

David rose from the table and smoothly acquired glasses and ice and poured tea without skipping a beat. He knew where everything was.

A couple of minutes later, they were all sitting at the table. The situation was bizarre, and Annie couldn't help feeling awkward as she sipped her tea. "So what can I do for you?"

Laura's forehead wrinkled with concern even as she smiled. "This is going to sound odd."

"Okay," Annie said. She took a bite of her sandwich while she waited for Laura to find the words she wanted.

"I originally asked David to do this, but we talked it over and thought that since you'd already met the girl, perhaps it would be better coming from you."

"What would be better coming from me?"

Laura sighed. She was clearly uncomfortable with what she was trying to say. Finally, she smiled again, this time with tears in her eyes. "Nick wanted children more than anything." She took another deep breath and closed her eyes to compose herself. "I'm sorry."

"Take your time," Annie said.

David put his hand over Laura's. "It's okay."

She squeezed his hand before clearing her throat and continuing. "Nick was an only child, and he just... he started a college fund. It was his thing. I didn't contribute. He told me I would have the babies and he would put them through college. But, of course, it didn't work out like that." She looked out the French doors at the massive deck and manicured lawn.

The silence went on for so long that Annie finished half her sandwich. Finally, she looked at David, who squeezed Laura's hand.

"Laura," he said gently.

Laura smiled weakly. "I'm sorry. So much has happened. Sometimes, it's a little overwhelming. Anyway, about the college fund, there's just over thirty thousand dollars in it. If this woman who says she's carrying Nick's baby would agree to a paternity test, then I'd be willing to put it in a trust to help pay for the baby to go to college."

Annie was stunned. "That's... wow... that's... very generous."

Laura closed her eyes again. "If Nick were still alive, I'm sure I'd feel differently, but if it's his child... I can give him this. I think it might, I don't know, give me some closure, maybe." David squeezed her hand again.

Annie cleared her throat. "There's just one problem."

Laura and David looked at her.

"She's in a coma."

"What?" David asked.

Laura shook her head. "I thought you just saw her."

"She fell down the stairs of her apartment building. The police are treating it as suspicious."

Laura gasped.

"That's terrible," David said, his brow wrinkling with concern.

"Who would do that to a pregnant woman?" Laura said.

"I don't know. The police are investigating," Annie said.

"What about the baby?" Laura asked.

"Alive, but it's kind of touch and go." Annie took a sip of her tea and watched their faces, looking for some inkling of guilt. Instead, all she saw was shock and confusion.

Laura looked alarmed. "Is this connected to Nick? Was she married? Did her husband go after them both?"

Annie shook her head. "No. She wasn't married and wasn't seeing anyone other than Nick, so far as I know. She told me she was married briefly several years ago, but her ex is in Arizona—married with a family."

"So it was unrelated," David said.

Annie shrugged. "So far, there's no connection, but one might turn up. It would be a very unusual coincidence if it weren't connected, assuming of course that it wasn't just an accident. The investigation is ongoing. Fairfax has lots of resources. They'll turn up something. They're keeping the Leesburg police in the loop, so if there is a connection, someone will find it."

Laura pressed a hand to her mouth and shook her head. Tears slipped down her cheeks as she stood and hurried upstairs.

Annie looked at David.

"This has been really hard on her," he said.

Annie decided to push him a little. "Of course it has, but she has you. I'm sure that helps."

He smiled, and a blush crossed his cheeks. "Is it that obvious?"

"Yes."

He sighed and turned his iced tea between his hands. "It's a cliché, I know, but we've known each other for a long time as friends, so it's not as tawdry as it seems."

Annie smiled and held up her hands. "Hey, no judgments here."

He chuckled softly. "I appreciate that. I'd like to think I'm not just a convenient port in a storm. She really loved Nick, despite his flaws." He frowned. "God knows why."

Annie took another sip of her tea. "She was planning to divorce him."

David smiled sadly. "Honestly, I think she was planning to threaten him with divorce."

"Seemed pretty serious to me."

David sighed. "Oh, she wanted her ducks in row, but I think she was hoping he'd see her side of it and change his behavior."

"Yeah, well, somebody changed it for him."

David nodded. "He's probably lucky someone didn't do it sooner."

Annie nodded. "Maybe if a few more guys had punched him in the mouth, he would have straightened out a long time ago."

David smiled. "Maybe so. But Nick lived a charmed life."

As she drove away, Annie had to agree with David. Nick had managed to get away with an awful lot for a really long time.

ON the drive back to Leesburg, Annie took a call from Gunnar. He asked her to come by the station. She longed to go home and sleep, but she drove past her apartment and took a right onto Loudoun Street instead. She went through the historic part of town until she reached Mom's Apple Pie Bakery, which sat on the corner where Loudoun Street and East Market Street merged. She thought briefly of stopping for pie but continued on. The historic district ended at Mom's. After that were mostly strip malls until she reached Plaza Street and took a left toward the police station.

When she walked in the front door of the modest brick building, Brian Rinker was the desk officer.

He grinned and said, "Hey, it's Little Big Man."

Annie smiled and rolled her eyes. At six feet eight, Gunnar had always been referred to as Big Man, so when Annie had been partnered with him, some of the guys thought it was hilarious to call her Little Big Man. The name had stuck.

"Hey, Brian," Annie said. "How's the workout going?"

Brian was a body builder. He puffed out his chest, straining the buttons on his uniform shirt. "Really good. What can I do for you today?"

"I'm just here to see Gunnar."

"Sure. Go on back," Brian said.

She made her way through the department, returning greetings and shaking hands and hugging the officers who were at the station doing paperwork rather than patrolling. When she finally reached Gunnar's cubicle, he was on the phone. He caught sight of her and motioned toward the conference room with his head. She went in to wait.

Annie couldn't help but be impressed when she opened the door. The conference room had been converted into a central office to process the murder of Nick Carlton. One wall was just four-by-six-inch photos of the women Nick had been with from the website. Several of the photos had Post-It flags indicating the dates they had been contacted and questioned and by whom and whether they had significant others and whether or not they had to be questioned further. Everything was color coded. Green meant they were cleared. Yellow ones needed follow-up. Red ones were people of interest. A lot of women were still on the board without flags. On another wall were closer associates of Nick's. Laura and Eddie and Susan figured most prominently, with information about their location on the night of the murder. Crime-scene photos were posted on another wall, and a computer on the conference table was running an animated scenario of the murder. Annie sat down and watched it while she waited for Gunnar.

The animation featured a nicely dressed tall white male, representing Nick, walking down an alley before being knocked in the head by a smaller figure in jeans and a hoodie. The second figure had nothing to indicate race or gender. It was just an outline of a person with the head concealed in the hoodie.

Gunnar came in a few minutes later, two cups of coffee in one hand and a pack of cookies in the other.

"This is impressive," Annie said, pointing at the computer, as he handed her one of the coffees and took a seat at the table.

"Yeah, the state boys set that up, but it hasn't done much in the way of solving the crime."

Annie sipped her coffee. "It'll be great for the trial, though."

Gunnar nodded. "Exactly." He opened the pack of cookies and held it out to her. "Want one?"

She declined. "Is that all you're eating these days? Snack-machine food?"

He looked sadly at the cookies, which looked dime-sized in his big hand. "For the most part."

Annie looked at the wall where Susan's picture was tacked to the board. "So how did the interview with Susan go?"

Gunnar leaned back in his chair and briefly closed his eyes. "Frustrating."

"So much for an easy confession."

Gunnar snorted. "Yeah, that didn't happen. Her attorney did most of the talking, but the truth is she doesn't have an alibi for the murder or for the night Jenny Tomlin took a tumble down the stairs."

"Well, that's good."

"It's neither good nor bad. I can't hold her. It's not illegal to be home alone. I have zero evidence to connect her to either crime scene. Her prints aren't on Nick's phone, and so far, they aren't in the stairwell at Jenny Tomlin's apartment building either. I don't have anyone or anything to place her at either scene. Fairfax wants to interview her, but she's one cool customer. I don't think they're going to get any further with her than I did."

"But you like her for this?" Annie said.

Gunnar frowned. "Honestly? No. I can't see a motive. It's not like she was in love with the guy. It sounds like it was an affair of convenience for her, just scratching an itch. She was just pissed off that he was scratching his itch with so many other women, so she called it off. She was angry because she saw him as reckless. She didn't want to be exposed to STDs and all that. I mean, I can kind of see her killing Nick if it had happened closer to the breakup or if he'd given her AIDS or even herpes or something, but why bash his head in months after the fact?"

"Festering resentment?" Annie ventured.

Gunnar shook his head. "I didn't sense any of that. She also legitimately didn't seem to know who Jenny Tomlin was. She didn't recognize any of the women we showed her, but she did know the name of the website he used. As much as I hate to say it, this might be exactly what she says it was."

"Even if she killed her husband?" Annie said. "What are the odds?"

Gunnar sighed. "I know, but the reality is there was no proof she killed her husband either. Although I think that's far more likely, if you read the file."

"And that doesn't seem odd to you?" Annie asked, arching an eyebrow at him.

"Of course it seems odd!" Gunnar said, his voice rising. He took a deep breath. "It's damned odd," he said, lowering his voice. "But 'damned odd' isn't something I can give the DA to take to court."

"So where does this leave the case?" Annie asked.

"It leaves us with dozens of other people to interview, but unless one of them confesses or their fingerprints match the phone or the stairwell, we've got a whole lot of nothing."

"Well, I have some news. It probably won't help, but at least it's new information."

Gunnar stared at her. "What new information?"

"Well, two things, really." She pulled out her phone and showed him the photo she'd taken of the business card in the flowers at the hospital and slid it over to him. "This coworker visited Jenny in the hospital. And Laura Carlton is sleeping with her lawyer."

Gunnar raised his eyebrows and slid the phone back to her. "Text me that. How long has the affair been going on?"

Annie shrugged. "It seems new, but there's also a third thing. Today, Laura wanted me to approach Jenny about having a paternity test."

"For what?"

"Nick apparently set up a college fund for future children. Laura's willing to put it in trust for the baby if it's really Nick's."

Gunnar raised his eyebrows. "Seriously? How much money are we talking about?"

"Thirty grand," Annie said.

He let out a low whistle. "Well, that's not nothing."

"She said it might give her closure to give away the money."

"Or assuage her guilt," Gunnar theorized.

Annie nodded. "Maybe, but we know for a fact that she didn't push Jenny Tomlin down the stairs."

Gunnar rubbed the stubble on his chin. "True, but what about her boyfriend?"

Annie nodded. "You might want to find out where he was when Nick was murdered too."

Gunnar raised his eyebrows. "Maybe I should."

Annie shrugged. "It's probably nothing."

"Probably, but we've interviewed most of the women in Loudoun and half the women in Fairfax along with their boyfriends, husbands, and lovers. Locating one lawyer on two nights should be a piece of cake."

Annie nodded and smiled at him. "True."

"Actually, while we're talking about interesting tidbits, guess whose mother was a Brickell," Gunnar said, arching an eyebrow.

"Brickell?" Annie didn't know what he was talking about.

"The guy with the oldest gravestone at the Old Stone Church," Gunnar said.

"Who's he related to?"

"Eddie Peabody," Gunnar said.

"That's crazy," Annie said. "So Eddie is connected to the murder weapon?"

"Yep," Gunnar said. "Tangentially, at least."

Annie shook her head. "Why would he have left the murder weapon on a family headstone?"

"Why indeed?"

Annie laughed. "You don't seriously think Eddie did it, do you? He's such a mewling little thing."

Gunnar shrugged. "You don't have to be big to knock someone out with a rock. What I do know is that he and Carlton were in business together, and there can be a lot of motives in that kind of partnership."

"Have the accountants come up with anything?"

Gunnar shook his head. "Not yet, but they're still going through files. They have a lot of clients and manage a lot of money."

"I don't know, Gunnar. None of my alarms went off when I talked to Eddie."

"No offense, Annie, but maybe your equipment is a little rusty."

She glared at him. "My equipment is just fine. Maybe you're just grasping at straws."

"Hey, come on," Gunnar said.

"You come on," Annie said. "You're telling me an intelligent, well-respected member of the community is smart enough to wear gloves when he clubs his best friend in the head but dumb enough to leave the murder weapon on the grave of his ancestor. Seriously?"

Gunnar frowned. "The way I see it, a rock to the head is not a pre-meditated way to kill someone. He was probably wearing gloves because it was cold, not to hide his fingerprints. And if he'd just knocked his best friend in the head with a rock, he was probably distraught and disoriented and maybe he went somewhere that made him feel grounded. Like his family's cemetery."

"I think you're reaching," Annie said, shaking her head.

"Of course I'm reaching. I don't have any solid evidence. I've never worked a case with fewer facts. I asked eighty people when Eddie got to the chamber-music event, and not a single one could give me an exact time. I looked through photos from the event, but the earliest ones

I see of Eddie were taken right on the line of when he could have been in Arlington before going to Oatlands. His fingerprints are on Nick's phone, but that doesn't mean anything because they worked together. And then there's your high-school theory. Eddie knew both Nick and Jenny from high school, but what does that mean?"

"Maybe it doesn't mean anything, or maybe it means everything," Annie said. "Maybe Eddie always had a crush on Jenny and was devastated to find out Nick got her pregnant. Maybe it's more about college, and Eddie always wanted Laura for himself. Maybe he freaked out because Nick really was going to California, and that was going to mess up the business. After all, Eddie said Nick was the one who brought in most of the clients."

Gunnar frowned. "So you think Eddie did it?"

Annie leaned back in her chair. "Not really, but let's say he did. How are you going to prove any of this?"

He pushed a hand back through his hair. "Hell if I know. But I think he needs to be questioned more extensively."

"Absolutely." Annie sighed. "This goes back to my point about high school, though. This is a weirdly tight little group. They're all up in each other's business."

Gunnar scratched at the stubble on his chin. "Then why don't they know who killed Nick?"

Annie raised her eyebrows at him. "Maybe they do."

<hr />

SEEING Gunnar had made Annie perk up and feel alert, but on the way back to her apartment, the exhaustion of having not slept the night before started to sink in again. Her hands were shaky from too much coffee, and she resolved to go home, take a shower, and lie down. Even if she couldn't sleep, she needed some rest. She was limping more and not thinking as clearly.

The shower was refreshing but did little to actually wake her. She crawled gratefully into bed just before noon, and Chester joined her, snuggling against her side. She closed her eyes, and the events of the past week floated to the surface as she dozed off. She thought about the Christmas fund-raiser and how much fun she'd had that night. She really needed to get out more. Unbidden, Eddie and Laura saying goodbye to everyone at the end of the event floated to the surface. She remembered Eddie resting his hand against the small of Laura's back and how quickly she'd rebuffed it. She thought about Eddie awkwardly working the crowd and how Miss Mabel had said he was always hanging around the big boys and how he was probably beside himself without Nick.

As she slipped into sleep, she dreamed of uneaten casseroles piling up in Laura's refrigerator, spilling out into the beautiful kitchen, filling up the house, and tumbling into the yard. The dream woke her slightly. She rolled over and wondered about Laura and Eddie and how they felt about each other. Maybe Eddie was just being a good Southern boy by bringing food to Laura, or maybe he felt responsible for her now that Nick was gone. Laura seemed resistant to that at the party, almost as though she didn't really like Eddie. Annie started to wonder about Nick and Eddie and what that relationship was all about. Ford had said Eddie was rumored to have done all of Nick's homework. She knew of only three reasons a kid would do that for another kid: he either was being strong-armed into it, was paid for it, or had a crush.

Annie sat up in bed. Maybe they'd been looking at Eddie's relationship with Nick all wrong. Gunnar had interviewed Eddie as Nick's business partner and had contracted with a forensic accountant to go through their books, but that was looking for money as a motive for murder, and they hadn't found anything. Maybe money wasn't Eddie's motive. He didn't have a solid alibi for Nick's murder. He'd said he was at Leesburg Brewing Company, but that was a busy night, and besides, it was Eddie's regular watering hole. He was there all the time.

The night of Nick's murder, the place was packed with people there to watch the game. No one could confirm exactly when Eddie got there or when he left, only that he was there that night. The same was true of the night someone threw Jenny Tomlin down the stairs. No one could say for sure what time Eddie had arrived at the fund-raiser, only that he had been there sometime before dinner. Eddie, of course, had said he'd gotten there way before dinner, but his arrival was a nonevent, so no one could remember it.

She reached for her phone, glancing at the time. It was one-thirty. Laura Carlton had known Eddie for years and should have had a good sense of how he felt about Nick. Annie wanted to talk to her, wanted to know how she thought Eddie would have reacted to Nick moving to California with Jenny Tomlin. Eddie claimed not to know about the pregnancy, but if he did know, he might have confronted Jenny. Maybe he wanted to scare her off, and when she didn't scare easily, he threw her down the stairs. It was hard to imagine Eddie doing that, though. The attack on Jenny didn't seem to fit. Perhaps it didn't. Laura picked up on the first ring.

"Hi, Laura," Annie said.

"Hello," Laura said. "Did that woman wake up?"

After a second, Annie realized Laura was talking about Jenny Tomlin. "No. Not that I've heard. Look, I know I just saw you this morning, but could we meet for coffee or something? I have some questions."

"I'm actually on my way into town right now to pick up some pictures from Nick's office. It looks like they're finally going to release the body so we can have a funeral. I wanted to make a couple of memory boards to put up on easels at the funeral home. I think people like those."

Annie agreed. "Yeah, those are nice. Can we meet before you go by there? It won't take long."

"Actually, I'm just now pulling in the driveway."

"That's okay," Annie said. "It's just a couple of blocks from me. I'll walk down. Would that be all right?"

"Sure. See you in a few," Laura said and hung up.

CHAPTER TWENTY
Saturday Afternoon

Annie rolled out of bed and pulled on her jeans. Chester got very excited.

"You're not going," Annie told him.

She slipped into her bra and pulled a sweatshirt over her head. Then she hurried to the door and put on her boots, not bothering with socks, and grabbed her coat. She stopped with her hand on the door-knob and looked at the table next to the door. If Eddie had snapped and killed Nick and tried to kill Jenny, she probably shouldn't go to his place without a weapon. On the other hand, she might be a lunatic imagining things. She opened the drawer and looked at her Sig Sauer P290. Then she sighed and closed the drawer. *It's not like I could shoot it if I had to.* Her hand still had a slight tremor, and she wasn't sure she could handle the weight of the trigger pull yet. The gun had been her backup piece when she was on the police force, but she didn't have a license to carry it concealed as a private investigator. She intended to do that when her hand was stronger. She closed the drawer. It would probably be overkill anyway. She locked the door behind her and started walking the two blocks to Eddie's house as quickly as she could. As the cold winter air cleared her head, the dreams slipped further and further away, and she felt as though she was on a fool's errand.

As she walked down Wirt Street, she heard a door slam and a man yell, "They're not yours to take!"

She heard Laura's voice shout back, "Don't be ridiculous! You'll get them back."

One of Eddie's neighbors, an older woman in a purple velour sweat suit, was taking out her trash. She looked at Annie, and they both approached the privacy fence that separated the two properties and peered over it.

Laura had a pile of picture frames in her arms. On top were the dueling pistols from the shelf behind Nick's desk.

"Dammit, Laura!" Eddie shouted, reaching for her. "Why do you always have to control everything?"

She pulled away from him as his hand closed around one of the pistols.

"These are mine too."

"Oh no," the neighbor standing next to her said. "I'm calling the police." She pulled a cell phone out of the front pocket of her hoodie and dialed 911.

Annie couldn't blame her, but at the same time, she had to wonder what the likelihood was that the pistols were loaded. She didn't think it was very likely. Besides, Eddie wasn't even holding it in the position to shoot. He was holding it by the barrel. She stepped partially from behind the fence and called Eddie's name.

But at the same time, Laura screamed, "How dare you?" which Annie thought was very bold and possibly very stupid. Eddie's face was red with fury, and while he might not have been able to shoot the gun while holding it like that, he could certainly club Laura in the face with it. Either way, Eddie hadn't heard Annie.

"Those are my pictures, and you better put them down," he said in a low voice, full of rage. He pointed at the ground with the pistol. "Put them down right now!"

"They're for the funeral. Don't you want Nick to have a decent funeral?" Laura's face was flushed, and the muscles in her jaw were clenching.

In the distance, Annie heard sirens.

But Eddie and Laura weren't listening.

"Why do you care about his funeral? You hired that woman to fol-low him." Eddie was still waving the gun around, using it to punctuate his sentences. "You wanted to divorce him."

"Eddie! Laura!" Annie shouted again, but neither one responded. She knew she was going to have to get closer if she wanted them to pay attention to her, but she didn't want to leave the meager protection of the fence if that old gun turned out to be loaded and Eddie decided to use it. Sweat was trickling down her back, but she felt chilled to the bone. She trembled, crouching behind the fence, and peered between the slats.

"And what possible business is that of yours?" Laura hissed.

Eddie's mouth dropped open. "You ruined everything!"

The sirens were getting closer.

"I wasn't the one that was cheating," Laura snapped.

"You knew what he was like when you married him," Eddie said, wiping tears from his face with the back of the hand holding the pistol. "He was leaving you and going to California. And that was your fault!" Eddie shouted, emphasizing the word "your" by thrusting the gun at her.

"Don't you mean 'us,' Eddie? He was going to leave us, you pathetic little man."

"He should have left you a long time ago," Eddie growled, pointing the gun's grip at Laura's face.

"No, Eddie. He should have left *you* a long time ago," Laura said, seemingly unfazed by the gun.

The sirens were so loud now that Annie knew the police were sec-onds from the scene. She stepped out from behind the fence, sweat trickling down her back and the scar on the side of her head burning. She felt stiff and anxious, as if her whole body was trying to keep her from moving.

"Put the gun down, Eddie!" Annie shouted, limping across the yard toward them. "Don't you hear the sirens?"

Eddie glanced in her direction as though noticing Annie for the first time. "Stay out of this!" he screamed. "This is none of your business."

"Oh my God," Laura gasped. "Did you kill him?"

Eddie whipped back around, his jaw dropped open in shock. "What? No!"

The first police car pulled onto the street.

"Eddie!" Annie shouted. "The cops are here. They'll shoot you if you don't put that gun down."

"Go away!" he screamed at her but turned his eyes back to Laura.

"Come on, Eddie. You don't want to do this," Annie pleaded.

But Eddie's focus was on Laura. He was crying. "My whole life..." His arms dropped to his sides, but he still had the gun in his hand.

"How could you?" Laura said.

Eddie was openly sobbing.

Annie heard car doors opening behind her. That sounded like at least two cars, but she was afraid to take her eyes off Eddie and Laura to look. She heard the first officer call for Eddie to drop the gun.

Eddie looked up, noticing the police for the first time. All the color drained from his face. He dropped the gun and raised his hands. He looked at Annie.

"What the hell is happening?" Laura said, her own face going pale as she put the pile of pictures on the ground and raised her hands as the police approached, guns drawn.

Annie turned around, raising her hands as well.

"Annie?" Mike Hartt said, lowering his gun. "What are you doing here?"

Another officer proceeded to pat down Eddie. "I wasn't doing anything," Eddie was saying. "This is my property."

"Laura is a client of mine," Annie told Mike. "I just walked over here to meet her."

"Look," Eddie said, regaining his composure and wiping his face, "I know what this looks like, but I wasn't going to hurt her. They're antiques, for God's sake."

"Uh-huh," the officer said.

"Laura, tell them!" Eddie shouted at her.

Laura said nothing.

"Those are my pistols and my photos," Eddie told the officers. "You should be arresting her for stealing them."

"Since when are they yours?" Laura sneered. "The guns were behind Nick's desk."

"Since always. They were behind Nick's desk because he had a shelf. They belonged to my grandfather." He turned to the officer. "See?"

Mike looked at Annie. "You know anything about these pistols?"

Annie shook her head. "Just that they were in the office. I don't know who they belonged to."

Behind Mike, another officer was talking to the neighbor.

Mike looked from Laura to Eddie to Annie. "You know what I think? I think we're going to resolve this down at the station."

"What?" Laura said, clearly shocked at the suggestion. "I can't do that. I have a funeral to plan."

"Well, ma'am, I think that's going to have to wait a bit. This gentleman is accusing you of stealing his property."

Laura flushed a furious red. "That 'gentleman' was just waving a gun around."

"And that's why we're taking him in for brandishing a firearm."

"Eddie! Tell them I wasn't stealing from you!" Laura shouted.

"Screw you," Eddie said. "This whole mess is your fault."

"This is ridiculous," Laura said, turning to the officer. "I need to call my lawyer."

"Oh, right, go running to that asshole," Eddie grumbled.

"You can call him from the station, ma'am," the officer informed her.

They were led to separate patrol cars.

"What about me?" Annie asked Mike.

"I'd appreciate it if you'd come down to the station to help sort this out."

She nodded. "Sure. I'll be down in a little while. I've just got to get my car."

Ford's colonial was closer to Eddie's house than Annie's apartment, so she walked the one block over to retrieve the 4Runner. She drove slowly to the police station, trying to work out what all this meant. She didn't understand the dynamics of Eddie and Laura's relationship or what Eddie meant in his comment about David. She felt like the answers were there but tantalizingly just out of reach.

WHEN she arrived at the police station, Laura and Eddie were already waiting in separate interview rooms.

Annie signed in at the desk and asked to speak to Gunnar. A few seconds later, he appeared in the lobby.

"Hey," Annie said.

"Hey yourself," Gunnar said. "What the hell?"

"Yeah, I don't know what's going on. Are they talking?"

Gunnar snorted. "Of course not. They've both called their lawyers, and we're waiting on their arrival."

"What about the guns?" Annie asked.

"Already checked. Firing pins have been removed, and the cylinders don't work."

"So Eddie was right. They weren't dangerous."

Gunnar smiled. "Not unless he was going to chuck one at her head. So while we're waiting, you want to tell me what happened?"

"What little I know, sure." Annie followed him to the conference room.

Gunnar poured them each a cup of coffee the consistency of motor oil and sat down at the long table.

Annie looked at the coffee. "How long has this been sitting on the warmer?"

"God only knows," Gunnar said and took a sip.

Annie left her cup untouched. Her tolerance for station coffee had rapidly diminished after she left the force.

"So," Gunnar prompted.

Annie explained about meeting Laura at Eddie's and the scene she walked up on.

Gunnar scrubbed a hand down his face. "So what did you want to ask Laura?"

Annie sighed. "I wanted to know if Eddie has a girlfriend or, more specifically, if he'd ever had a girlfriend."

Gunnar raised an eyebrow at her. "Why?"

"Ford said the rumor in high school was that Eddie did all of Nick's homework. I only know of three reasons he would have done that."

"Money, love, or coercion," Gunnar said.

"From what I know about his family, it doesn't seem like he would need money. And if he was coerced, why did they remain friends after school?" Annie said.

"You think Eddie might have been in love with Nick all these years?"

Annie shrugged. "Maybe. Or maybe he just idolized him. Who knows, but I think it's worth finding out."

"That would give him a motive if he knew Nick really was planning to go to California," Gunnar mused.

"Sure, and he told Laura that was going to happen when they were arguing today."

Gunnar nodded. "Okay."

Mike stuck his head in the conference room. "Gunnar, the lawyers are here."

Gunnar stood. "Do you mind hanging around for a while?"

"Sure," Annie said.

She sat in the conference room for a few minutes and contemplated actually drinking the coffee but thought better of it. She walked back down the hall and told the desk sergeant she'd be back in a few minutes. As she walked to the 4Runner to go get coffee, David and Laura stepped out of one of the interview rooms.

"They released you," Annie said. "Great."

"Eddie finally told them I wasn't trying to steal from him."

David's jaw twitched. "At least that little weasel did something right."

Annie nodded. "You should get some rest. I'll call you later, okay?"

Laura nodded.

David wrapped a protective arm around her shoulders and led her toward his car. "Why don't you stay with me tonight?"

Laura nodded.

Annie watched them walk to the car for a moment before heading to the 4Runner.

AS she drove toward McDonald's, she changed her mind about the coffee and went to Ford's house instead. Once inside, she went upstairs to the spare bedroom he used as an office. There on the bottom of a bookshelf were his high-school yearbooks. She pulled out the one from his freshman year since it was the only one that would feature Nick and Eddie. She wasn't sure what she was looking for—probably not a picture of them surreptitiously holding hands or something to offer proof of Eddie's affections—but she couldn't help feeling as though something was missing, and all roads seemed to lead to high school.

The book opened with a dedication to a dead student. She had curly red hair, big blue eyes, and a bright smile, and her name was Stephanie Cohen. Annie wondered if she was related to David Cohen.

The dedication was a poem, but it didn't say anything about how the girl had died.

Annie flipped to the back of the book and looked up Eddie and then Nick in the index. They were in a lot of the same club pictures. To her surprise, David Cohen also appeared in those pictures. Nick was student-body president. David was vice president. Eddie was secretary. Nick was the star quarterback. David was the backup. Eddie was the team manager. Nick was the Key Club president. David was the vice president. Once again, Eddie was the secretary. The list went on for half a dozen other clubs and sports. The only exception was valedictorian. Eddie was valedictorian. David was salutatorian. Nick didn't rank. Annie pushed the book away and leaned back in her chair for a moment.

It seemed like too much of a coincidence that Cohen was now dating his high-school rival's wife. On the other hand, it also seemed ridiculous that it would matter so many years later. Annie frowned. Maybe Gunnar was right, and her skills were rusty. Surely, David couldn't have killed Nick over jealousy, not all these years later. That was absurd. She flipped back to the photo of Stephanie Cohen.

Curious, she took her phone out of her pocket and typed Stephanie's name, the year, and "death" into Google's search box. Unfortunately, nothing relevant came up. Her first instinct was to check police records, but she didn't have access to those, and she didn't want to send Gunnar on a wild goose chase for records that old, which might not even be digitized yet.

She knew the Thomas Balch Library had the local paper archived back more than a century. She checked their hours on her phone and saw they were open.

She called the police station.

The desk officer answered.

"Hey, Brian, could you let Gunnar know I have to run an errand? I'll give him a call later."

"No problem, Annie. I'll let him know."

"Thanks." She ended the call, took a picture of the yearbook dedication page, and headed to the library.

ANNIE parked the 4Runner in the tiny lot behind the library and
walked in through the new addition at the rear of the building.

A tall man with snow-white hair was at the information desk talking to someone on the phone about historic land grants. Annie passed
the time looking at the mural that wrapped the top wall of the atrium.

A couple of minutes later, the man hung up the phone and smiled
at Annie. "How can I help you?"

Annie smiled back. "I'm kind of stuck. I'm trying to find out how
someone local died. I was thinking maybe the newspaper might have
an obituary. The problem is the death occurred in 1997."

"We have the paper archived on microfilm for the nineties."

"Is there an index? I'm not sure exactly what day or month she died,
only that it was 1997."

He gave her a sympathetic look. "Sadly, no. I'm afraid you'll have to
scroll through the whole year. It shouldn't be too bad, though. It's only
three rolls of microfilm per year, and most of it you can skim through."

Annie nodded. "Okay."

He took her to the center of the library, where the microfilm was
stored in cabinets, and pulled the spools for 1997. Annie took a seat
and proceeded to thread the microfilm onto the machine. Toward the
end of the third reel, she found Stephanie Cohen's obituary listing her
parents and twin brother, David, as surviving her. She backed up a bit,
scanning the paper more carefully and was rewarded with an article.
Four high-school seniors on their way to a party from a football game
were T-boned at an intersection by a drunk driver. Nick Carlton had
been driving. Stephanie Cohen was sitting in the passenger's seat. Eddie Peabody and another boy named Carl Shortz had been seated in
the back. Eddie was sitting behind Nick. Carl was behind Stephanie.

When Nick took a left at a light, the other driver had blown through the red light at top speed, hitting the passenger side of the car. Stephanie was pronounced dead at the scene. Carl had gone to the hospital with life-threatening injuries and died later. Nick and Eddie had been treated for minor injuries. The drunk driver hadn't been wearing a seat belt. Like Stephanie, he'd been pronounced dead at the scene. Annie read the article again to make sure she hadn't missed something. Nick wasn't charged, and nothing about alcohol was mentioned on his part. The crash was an accident caused by the other driver. Annie sat back and looked at the screen.

Maybe she was barking up the wrong tree. Cell-phone use was banned in the library, which she generally appreciated, but not today. She rewound the microfilm, turned off the machine, and returned the spools to the librarian before walking out to the parking lot to call Laura.

LAURA answered on the first ring.

"Hey," Annie said. "I just wanted to see if you were doing okay." She opened the car door and slid in out of the cold.

Laura sighed. "I'm fine. This whole thing is ridiculous. When David gets back with lunch, I'm going to talk to him about Eddie. We can't let the cops bully him. Eddie didn't kill Nick any more than I did."

"I don't think the cops are bullying Eddie, Laura. He's a person of interest because he was Nick's business partner, and that stunt at his house with the gun didn't help his cause. That's all." Annie started the car, and the phone switched over to the Bluetooth speaker.

"The gun wasn't loaded. It can't even fire. Those things were disabled ages ago. He would never keep real guns on display in his office. Eddie can be annoying, but he's not an idiot."

"I know," Annie said.

"So what did you want to ask me?" Laura asked, yawning.

"Did Eddie ever have designs on you, make a drunken pass, anything like that?"

Laura laughed. "Eddie? No. I'm not even sure Eddie is attracted to women. If you ask me, Nick was the great love of Eddie's life, which is probably why we get on each other's nerves so much. In the end, Ed and I have more in common than either of us would like to admit."

"So Eddie and Nick..." Annie backed out of the parking lot and turned to take a left on Market Street back toward her apartment.

Laura laughed again. "No. It was strictly one-sided. Although, to be honest, I think Nick used Eddie's affections to manipulate him more often than he should have. Nick could be a jerk that way, but if he noticed, Eddie never seemed to mind."

Annie thought for a second. Eddie had a strong motive if he was in love with Nick since he knew Nick was planning to move to California with Jenny. Annie filed that away for a moment and changed tactics. "What about David? Did he ever talk about Nick?"

"No. Why would he?" Laura yawned again.

Annie paused. "Did David ever mention he went to school with Nick and Eddie?"

"He did?"

"Yes. The three of them are all over their high-school senior yearbook. They were all very active." Annie took a right on Liberty Street.

"When have you seen David's yearbook?" Laura sounded confused.

"I haven't. I've seen my boyfriend's yearbook. His freshman year was Nick and David's senior year."

"I had no idea. God, I'm so tired."

"I'm sure. You've had a really rough week," Annie said. "Look, I know David's gone to get lunch, but there are some things I'd really like to go over with you. Do you think I could come over now, and we could cover some of this stuff?"

"Like what?" Laura asked.

"Like has David ever mentioned his sister?"

Laura paused on the other end of the line. "He has a picture of her on his mantel. She died quite young, in a car accident, I think."

"Did he tell you Nick was driving the car she was in when she died? Did he mention Eddie was in the car, too, along with another boy named Carl, who also died?"

"No. I mean, I think he said their cousin Carl died in the same accident. He was in town visiting or something. He's never said anything about Nick or Eddie being in the car. Are you sure?" Laura's voice was starting to sound thick, and she was answering more slowly.

"Did Nick and David ever have any interactions that you were aware of?"

Laura paused again. Annie drove through the parking lot at the end of Liberty Street and down S Street toward King. She wasn't sure which house was David's, but she knew he lived past the Battery Warehouse in one of the big houses that hadn't been converted into a business yet on that part of King Street.

"They were both on the board of the Chamber Music Association. They didn't really get along. David was always really nice to me. I think Nick was a little jealous." She giggled.

"Laura," Annie said. "Is your car still at Eddie's?"

"Yes. David brought me here."

"Okay. I'm on my way to you. I know he's on King Street, but which house is David's?"

Laura yawned again. "I've got to get some sleep."

"Which house, Laura?" Annie insisted.

"The white one... with the porch," she said, her words slightly slurred.

CHAPTER TWENTY-ONE
Late Saturday Afternoon

Annie parked behind a Honda Odyssey on the opposite side of King Street from a large, two-story white house with a front porch and a balcony above that. Over the last century, the house had been expanded to fill most of the back of its lot. Annie hurried forward to ring the bell. No one answered. She looked through the windows on either side of the door and saw Laura asleep on the sofa. She was barefoot and wearing black yoga pants and a pink T-shirt with Namaste printed on it.

Annie leaned on the doorbell with her right index finger and banged on the door with her left hand while she yelled Laura's name.

Finally, Laura opened her eyes. She was making a huge effort to get off the sofa and shuffle to the front door. She opened it but just a crack. Annie pushed her way inside.

Laura didn't seem upset by the rudeness or even fully aware of it. She headed back for the sofa.

Annie grabbed her arm, "Hey, we need to go."

"Too sleepy. Need to lay down." Obviously, Laura had taken something that was knocking her out.

"What did you take?"

"Nothing. David got me some aspirin. So tired."

Immediately suspicious, Annie barked at her, "Put your shoes on!"

"But I don't—"

"Now!" Annie shouted. "Go get your coat and shoes right now." She wasn't sure exactly what was going on, but it didn't seem good.

Laura seemed to finally hear her and walked toward the back of the house. Annie followed her down a long dark hallway, resisting the urge to hurry her along. As she walked, she texted Gunnar, knowing he wouldn't take a call during an interview but desperately hoping he'd glance down at a text. She typed, "Cohen drugged Laura. Need you at house ASAP!" Then she typed the address. She looked around. The décor was all very masculine. As they walked by a door that opened off the hallway, Annie saw what looked like a home office with a mounted bear head on the wall behind a large mahogany desk.

Another room had more taxidermy, this time of several different types of birds realistically arranged on a large branch affixed to the wall. A bed was also in the room. Annie thought that seemed very creepy for a guest room. She got more and more nervous as they moved through the house. A few other doors along the central hallway were closed. When they passed a bathroom, Annie stepped in to find a bottle of aspirin next to a prescription bottle of Klonopin on the vanity. She grabbed both bottles and stuffed them into her coat pocket.

Laura's shoes were in a back den with a large sofa done in a Scottish tartan. An enormous flat-screen TV was mounted on the wall in front of it, and a small fridge served as an end table. Some kind of animal documentary was playing on the TV, but the sound was muted. *Man cave,* Annie thought, but the whole house seemed like a man cave to her. She watched from the doorway as Laura sat down on the sofa to put on her shoes. She tried to think of a benign reason David Cohen would have drugged Laura without her knowledge. Nothing came to mind. Laura's mental state was inhibiting the shoe thing. She stared off into space, one shoe partially on.

"Good grief," Annie said and knelt to put on Laura's shoes. Just as Annie finished tying them, she heard the front door open.

"Laura?" David called from the front of the house. "I've got lunch."

Laura looked up at Annie. "Not hungry. You hungry?"

If the situation hadn't felt so crazy, Annie would have laughed. Even on Klonopin, Laura was a good host.

"No, I'm good," Annie whispered. "Is there a back door?"

"Side door."

"Okay, we're going to head for that." Annie's heart was pounding.

"Why?" Laura asked thickly.

"We've got to go." All the additions on the old house had chopped it up weirdly. She stood, but Laura seemed glued to the sofa. "Come on," Annie hissed through gritted teeth and grabbed Laura's hand.

"Laura? Are you sleeping?"

Laura started to answer, but Annie pressed a finger to her lips and tried to get her up off the sofa.

Annie could hear David Cohen walking through the house, his footsteps creaking on the hardwood floors.

She finally got Laura up, but when she turned, David was standing at the door of the den, a brown paper bag in his hand.

He looked at Annie, confusion registering on his face, and then he smiled. "You were shot in the head. I figured it was safe to hire you."

"I got better," Annie said, far more glibly than she felt.

David's eyes flicked to Laura, who was barely able to stand on her own. He locked eyes with Annie. Then everything happened at once. David dropped the bag of food and turned to run down the hall. Annie desperately hoped he was running to his car to drive away, but she couldn't count on that. She grabbed Laura's arm and ran down the hallway. She hadn't seen an exit on the left side of the house as she'd walked in from her car, so she searched for an exit on the right. She found one in the middle of the hallway. She hadn't noticed it before because it looked like a small closet, but it was actually a small hallway off the main hall that had a weird dogleg turn in it. She was pushing Laura in front of her toward the door when she heard David coming up behind them. At least Laura had the presence of mind to open the door.

Annie pushed her out as she heard a thundering blast. She felt a burning pain in her shoulder as the doorjamb next to her blew apart. Annie slammed the door behind her, hoping to slow him down, and ran to help Laura, who had fallen on her hands and knees. Annie's ears were ringing as she pulled Laura to her feet. Images flashed in her mind. She was running in another neighborhood with other gunshots. Pushing down the panic, she tried to focus on the situation at hand.

She ran blindly across the street despite the increasing afternoon traffic, dragging Laura with her. Her right leg was screaming with the effort. She found a break in the line of cars and pushed Laura behind a Honda Odyssey and fell on top of her just as the back window blew out, showering glass over both of them. Annie stayed low but chanced a quick peek through the car's side windows. David was standing on the porch, the shotgun broken open. He was reloading with shells from his pockets. Annie was grateful the shotgun was a fancy over/under model instead of a semiautomatic that would hold several shells at a time. She could hear sirens coming toward them.

Laura's eyes were huge and dilated despite the bright afternoon sunlight. "He's trying to kill us. Why is he doing that?"

Annie took a deep breath. The pain in her shoulder was searing, but she resisted the urge to look to see how bad it was. She tucked her right hand into her coat pocket to try to take the weight of her arm off her shoulder. The first patrol car pulled up, blocking the street at an angle well away from David's house. Moments later, another patrol car did the same thing on the other side, so King Street was completely blocked off.

"Let's stay here," Annie said. "This is pretty good cover, and running would expose us."

Laura yawned again as she nodded. She didn't seem to notice that she'd torn her yoga pants when she'd fallen and that her palms and knees were skinned.

Annie couldn't stop shaking. Her phone rang. Gunnar was calling. He said something, but she was having trouble hearing over the ringing in her ears.

"Where are you?" Gunnar shouted again.

"I'm behind the red minivan across from Cohen's house," Annie said.

"Do you have Laura Carlton?"

"Yes."

"Are you both okay?"

Annie paused. "Mostly. When you can get an ambulance safely in here, that would be good."

"Shit!" Gunnar said. "Hang tight."

ANNIE peeked again and saw that David was no longer on the porch. She really hoped he'd gone back inside to put down the gun and the situation could be resolved quickly. She looked around as more squad cars arrived. Officers got out of their cars and took positions of cover behind them. Other officers farther back were rerouting traffic. Everyone was wearing bulletproof vests and helmets and carrying tactical weapons. Annie wished she had the same equipment. Behind the police line, Dawn Sullivan was wearing her royal-blue trench coat. *Oh great. Now the nightmare circle of this day is complete.*

Annie looked over at Laura, who was slumped forward with her eyes closed. She peered around the corner of the car. She could see Gunnar on his cell phone. Weirdly, he started moving toward her, keeping as low as he could and staying behind the cars. When he reached the minivan, he crouched next to her and Laura.

"Cohen called us. He says he'll only talk to you. I talked to the captain. He's okay with that if you are."

Annie sighed and took the phone and held it to her left ear. "David, it's Annie."

He said something she couldn't make out.

"You're going to have to speak up, David. I can't hear very well right now."

"I'm sorry I shot you," David said. He actually sounded sorry.

"Yeah," Annie said, smiling at the absurdity of the situation, despite the burning pain in her shoulder. "I wish that hadn't happened too. Why don't you put the gun down and come on out with your hands up so no one else gets hurt."

David continued as if Annie hadn't said anything. He sounded oddly calm. "This is all Nick's fault."

"Okay," Annie said soothingly. "How's that?" She began to shiver and clenched her teeth to keep them from chattering.

Gunnar pulled off his heavy woolen coat and draped it over her like a blanket.

"He told me what he was planning to do to that poor girl that night in the alley. He wanted legal advice on paternity. He wanted to see if he could get custody of the child and keep her from taking it to California. Can you believe that? What a monster. And he wanted free legal advice from me. Me. Like I'd somehow forgotten who he was, like I would help him take that woman's baby. You know, I tried to tell her exactly what kind of guy he was, but she wouldn't believe me." He didn't continue.

"And then she fell down the stairs," Annie prompted.

"I never touched her. I called her to tell her about Nick."

"So your phone number will appear on her phone?" Annie said keeping her voice calm.

"I keep a prepaid burner phone for dealing with difficult clients."

Annie resisted the urge to ask about that. "Well, she's still alive, and her baby is still alive, so you're okay on that. Why don't you come outside now? Put your gun down and your hands up, and show the police you're not the bad guy here."

"I was never the bad guy," David said. "Nick was the bad guy. He was always the bad guy. Why did no one ever see that?"

"It's unfair," Annie agreed. She looked at Gunnar.

Gunnar made a circular motion with his finger for her to keep him talking. Sharpshooters were taking position in case Cohen decided to come out shooting. The pain in her shoulder was worsening, and her leg was in agony from the strain of crouching, so she repositioned herself to sit on the ground.

"Everything has gone awry," he said, his voice cracking. He cleared his throat.

"It's not too late to pull it back, David."

"Yes it is. It's way past too late. He did the same thing to my sister, you know, just like that Tomlin girl. He got her pregnant. Of course, he didn't want a baby back then, so he killed her."

"I thought that was an accident," Annie said.

Cohen let out a sharp, bitter laugh. "He was drinking. I know he was drinking."

"You saw him that night?"

"Sure, at the game. But he was going to a party, so I know he must have been drinking. I told Stephanie not to go, but she was so impressed with precious Nick Carlton that she wouldn't listen. She was sure he loved her. She never did accept the truth about him. Carl tried to calm me down by saying he'd go with her, but all that did was get him killed too. I know Nick only ever asked her out to get under my skin. Then that bastard got her killed." He didn't sound angry as much as resigned.

"I'm sure a judge will understand that, David. Come on out, and tell your side to the police. They'll understand. They know what kind of man he was. They've been interviewing all those women."

"You really surprised me," David said, ignoring her suggestion again. "Who knew you'd still be a decent investigator after being shot in the head?"

"It was a glancing blow," Annie said to keep him talking, "but it still took a long time to recover. It's not something I'd care to repeat or recommend for anyone else."

"Yes, you've got to make sure you're square on the target if you want to stop the clock."

"David," Annie said again, "put the gun down, and come on out."

"I'm a lawyer," David said wistfully. "My life is over."

"That's not true, David. You know and I know nothing is set in stone. You get a good lawyer. You tell your side. A jury can be very sympathetic. You've never hurt anyone before. No one is going to throw the book at you. Put the gun down and come out."

"I can't," he said softly.

A deafening explosion sounded, and Annie jerked the phone away from her ear. Everyone had heard it.

"Dammit," Gunnar said.

For a moment, everyone was still. Then police officers cautiously moved forward. After a minute, an officer with a bulletproof shield breached the porch and looked through a window. He signaled all clear, and everyone moved at once. The ambulances that had been waiting outside the police perimeter were let through. One set of paramedics went into the house with the police, and Gunnar waved the second set of paramedics to check on Annie and Laura. Laura was slumped over, unconscious.

Gunnar helped Annie to her feet.

"Hey," Annie said to one of the paramedics, "I think he drugged her with these." She handed him the Klonopin and aspirin bottles.

"I'll catch up with you at the hospital," Gunnar said.

Annie got to her feet and handed Gunnar back his coat. She began shrugging her own coat off her left arm. The young paramedic helped her slide it off her right arm.

"How's the pain?" he asked.

"It hurts, but the doorjamb took the brunt of the blast."

"All right, let's get you in the ambulance and take a better look."

"Annie! Annie!" Dawn Sullivan was shouting.

A police officer was keeping her back. Next to her, a photographer was steadily snapping photos.

One medic took Annie's vitals on her left arm while the other cut away her shirt from the right. Annie looked out the back of the ambulance as Laura, supported by a paramedic, stood in the middle of the road, the lights from the police cars, ambulances, and fire engines swirling around her. As they were pulling away from the curb, Annie saw the medic helping her into another ambulance.

CHAPTER TWENTY-TWO
Saturday Evening

Sometime later, Gunnar found her in the emergency room on Cornwall Street. Annie was having the birdshot removed from her numbed right shoulder by a Dr. Rajan, who looked as though she had just graduated from high school instead of medical school. Luckily, she was more skilled than her youth implied, and aside from the sting of the shots to numb her shoulder, Annie wasn't feeling too bad.

Gunnar, on the other hand, was gray-faced, and his brow was creased with worry. "Hey, how are you?"

"Pretty good," Annie said. "I'm lucky Cohen liked to shoot birds instead of deer. Besides, he basically missed me. There are only eleven pellets in my arm. She doesn't think they hit anything vital."

Gunnar looked at the doctor for confirmation.

"She'll be sore and will probably need some physical therapy when the wounds heal, but there shouldn't be any lasting damage."

"So... way better than the last time I got shot," Annie quipped, trying to lighten Gunnar's mood.

He frowned at her.

"Come on, Gunnar," she said, tugging his sleeve with her good hand. "I'm okay."

He sighed.

Annie blinked back tears and cleared her throat to stave off the lump trying to form. "So did you release Eddie?"

He nodded. "He's actually down the hall with Laura. She's still sleeping off the Klonopin, which is probably a blessing, given the day's events. They're keeping her for observation."

201

"I'll check on her before I leave."

"Have you called your dad?" Gunnar asked.

"Um, no." Annie grimaced. "I'm not up for that just yet. He's going to flip his lid. I'll call him tonight. Celia's on her way to take me home."

"I could have done that," Gunnar said.

"I didn't want to ask. I know you've got a mountain of paperwork."

Gunnar sighed again. "Yeah."

Dr. Rajan put another bandage on her shoulder. "We're all done here."

"Annie?" Celia called from the other side of the curtain.

"I'm in here," Annie said.

Celia stepped in. Her lips were in a tight line, and her eyes were red, but she was holding it together. "How are you doing?"

"I'm okay."

Celia nodded. "Good. I brought you a flannel shirt and a coat. They're mine, so they'll be a little big, but I thought that might be better since you'd have a bandage."

"Thanks," Annie said.

Gunnar cleared his throat and stood to leave. "I should get going so you can get dressed. Call me tomorrow. I'll come by then and get your statement."

"Thanks, Gunnar," Annie said. "I'll see you tomorrow."

After Gunnar walked out, Celia hugged Annie's left side and Annie leaned her head against her.

"I'm okay," she said again.

Celia nodded and wiped her eyes. "I left a message with the emergency contact for Ford. They said they wouldn't be able to reach him for a few days." She helped Annie get dressed.

An orderly showed up with a wheelchair, and they slowly made their way down the hall toward the entrance. They passed Laura's room. She was still sleeping, and Eddie was in a chair next to her bed, looking at his phone. He didn't look up as they passed, so Annie didn't bother him.

CELIA insisted Annie come home with her for the night. They stopped at Annie's apartment to pick up Chester and then at CVS to fill Annie's prescription for pain before heading to Purcellville. Annie's leg was very stiff, and she was limping worse than she had in months as she walked into the house. Celia fussed over her the rest of the evening. They had hot cocoa to chase away the chill and then roast chicken and succotash for dinner. They watched *The Princess Bride*. Annie was grateful for the distraction and grateful that Celia didn't press her for all the details she must have wanted to know. She planned on telling her, just not then. After dinner, Annie couldn't keep her eyes open, so Celia set her up in the guest room under flannel sheets and a beautiful heavy woolen afghan that Celia had crocheted herself.

Annie had a fitful night, though. The wounds on her shoulder made it difficult to sleep despite the Tylenol #3. When she did manage to doze off, she dreamed of the day's events interspersed with flashes of the last time she'd been shot. She still didn't have a full memory of that event, but vague pieces were there where none had been before. Whenever she woke, Chester was there to lick her hand or snuggle against her. Annie was ever so grateful for the little guy and held him close.

CHAPTER TWENTY-THREE
Sunday Morning

At six o'clock in the morning, she awoke in tears. David Cohen killing himself after shooting at her... Ford leaving... Everything was too much. She heard Celia puttering around in the kitchen, so she went to wash her face and join her.

Celia's Dobermans were both sitting in rapt attention as Celia made breakfast. Chester sat next to them, sure that they wouldn't be sitting so still if treats were not forthcoming. When the bacon and eggs were done, each dog was rewarded for good behavior with a piece of bacon.

"You shouldn't give Chester a whole piece," Annie said. "He's little."

"Sorry," Celia said, setting a plate in front of her. "I forget. I don't usually even make bacon, which is why these two are so excited."

"Thanks for making breakfast and for letting me stay here last night."

"Anytime," Celia said, smiling.

Annie looked at the perfectly cooked bacon and eggs. "You shouldn't spoil me. I might never leave."

"If you stay, you have to learn to knit."

Annie raised her eyebrows in mock alarm. "I should probably go home today."

"See, no worries."

Annie chuckled.

Gunnar called during breakfast and said he would come out to get her statement. He was there in half an hour, and Celia poured them all coffee.

"Guess who's awake," Gunner said with a smile.

"Laura or Jenny Tomlin?" Annie said.

"Both. But I was mostly talking about Tomlin. She and her baby seem like they're going to be okay."

"Oh thank goodness," Annie said with a sigh of relief.

"But the weird thing is she confirmed that she just slipped."

"Seriously?" Annie said. "What kind of crazy coincidence is that?"

Gunnar shook his head. "I know. What are the odds?"

"So Cohen was telling the truth on that. Go figure."

"I wonder if Laura Carlton will still be willing to put that money in trust for Tomlin's baby," Gunnar said.

Annie raised her eyebrows. "I don't know, but I think so."

Celia nodded. "I bet she sees it as a way to put all of this behind her."

"Maybe so," Gunnar said. "Are you ready to give me your statement?"

"Yes," Annie said, eager to get it over with.

She smiled, and Gunnar pulled out his notepad. Annie asked Celia to stay for the statement so she didn't have to repeat it all later. She walked through the events of the day with as much detail as she could.

When she was done, Gunnar shook his head. "What the hell was wrong with Cohen? Why would he throw his life away like that?"

"I guess he didn't want to go to prison. I can't say as I blame him."

"Yeah, I get that," Gunnar said. "But why did he kill Nick in the first place?"

"Nick got his sister pregnant in high school, and then he was driving the car his sister died in. Cohen and his sister were twins. He never got over it."

"And it took him twenty years to exact his revenge? What the hell?" Gunnar grimaced.

"I think when Nick approached him in the alley to ask about his legal options with Jenny Tomlin, it brought it all back, and Cohen snapped. It seemed like he was pretty high-strung. That Klonopin pre-scription was his, and he was on a pretty high dose."

Gunnar scrubbed a hand down his face. "I didn't even think to look at him."

"Why would you?" Annie asked. "He was her lawyer and seemingly unconnected to Nick. If I hadn't bothered to look through Ford's year-books, I never would have made the connection either, which makes me wonder: if I hadn't gone over to get Laura, what would have hap-pened? Did he intend to hurt her? Or would he have returned to his normal life as if a great injustice had finally been righted, and he could now go about his life, enjoying what should have been his all along?"

"I don't think so," Celia said. "Guys like that always have a reason to snap. She might have been safe with him for a little while, but eventu-ally he would have turned on her. She's lucky you showed up when you did and got her out of there."

"She's right," Gunnar said.

Annie shook her head in disbelief. "Why drug her then?"

Gunnar shrugged. "Who knows?"

"He might have seen it as a kindness," Celia said. "You know, to calm her down."

Annie grimaced. "Without telling her?"

"If he thought that's what she needed, he probably wouldn't have asked. Control freaks are all assholes," Celia said with a conviction that made Annie sad.

"Have you seen the paper yet this morning?" Gunnar asked.

Celia shook her head. "I haven't brought it in."

"You might want to take a look," Gunnar said. "This was a big story. Lots of pictures. I'm guessing it's in the *Post* too."

Annie sighed. If the story had made the *Washington Post*, her father would see it. She'd turned her phone off last night, but she went to get it while Celia went to fetch the paper.

When she returned to the table, Gunnar was finishing his coffee, and Celia had the paper. She handed it to Annie. The entire front page was about yesterday's events on King Street. A photo showed the chaos of the entire scene. Another photo showed Gunnar leaning over her, looking very protective as she talked with Cohen on the phone, and yet another photo showed her in the back of the ambulance. Amid all that was an incongruous professional portrait of David Cohen and another of Nick Carlton. She didn't have the stomach to read the article yet.

"Great," she said. She looked down at her phone—twenty-five missed calls. "Just great."

CHAPTER TWENTY-FOUR
Two Days before Christmas, Late Morning

After an extended cold snap, temperatures in the upper forties seemed warm, so Annie sipped her latte in one of the red Adirondack chairs outside King Street Coffee and reveled in the sunshine on her face. Beside her, Chester crunched a treat the barista had given him from a glass jar on the counter. Annie was tired from physical therapy on her shoulder, but at least her leg seemed better again. If only the rest of her life would go back to normal. She was tired of sleeping alone and wished Ford would come back from wherever he was. She closed her eyes for a moment and tried to clear her mind and just enjoy the sunshine.

Chester let out a happy bark and squirmed at the end of his leash, wagging his tail. Annie looked up to see a man approaching. For a moment, she didn't recognize Ford. He had a full beard, and his thick, brown hair was slicked back and longer than he usually kept it. One arm was tucked inside his Navy peacoat, so his left sleeve swung empty. Aside from the empty sleeve, he could have been a model for some manly product like cigars or bourbon. Her breath caught at the sight of him.

"Hey," he said as he approached her. His voice was deep and more gravelly than normal, as though he was recovering from a sore throat.

"You're back." She stood to give him a hug.

They held each other for a long time, and she breathed in the spicy scent of him. When they finally parted, Ford scooped up Chester with his good arm and sat down in another Adirondack chair next to Annie.

Chester promptly rooted his nose into Ford's beard and began sniffing. Ford chuckled and put the little dog back on the ground.

He smiled at Annie. "Things wrapped up sooner than expected."

Annie didn't bother asking what things he was referring to. "What'd you do to your arm?"

"It's broken."

Annie noted the nonanswer. She wondered if he'd had an accident or if someone had broken it for him. She didn't ask. He wouldn't tell her anyway.

"How's your shoulder?" he asked.

"Better. Still in PT, but it's going well," she said with false cheer.

"Good." He looked at her intently.

She glanced away from the intensity of his stare. "Are you home for Christmas?"

He smiled. "Yep." Then his face turned serious. "You got shot again."

"Glancing blow," she said.

His jaw twitched. "That's what you said last time."

"This time is better." She smiled at him.

He didn't smile back. "I'd prefer it not happen again."

She shrugged her left shoulder. "Me too."

"So?" He glared at her.

The question hung in the air. She knew he and her father wanted her to quit being a private investigator.

Annie had no plans to quit, so she shifted the conversation. "So, how'd you break your arm?"

His mouth tightened, but he didn't respond. They stared into each other's eyes for a long moment, each assessing the other's willpower and neither one yielding.

"So, breakfast?" Ford asked.

"Brunch, really, at this time of day," Annie observed.

"You in?"

"Absolutely."

He took her hand, and they made their way down the street, putting off big conversations until another day.

Dear Reader,

We hope you enjoyed *Exposed Fury*, by Marie Flanigan. Please consider leaving a review on your favorite book site.

Visit our website[1] to sign up for the Red Adept Publishing Newsletter to be notified of future releases.

---

1. http://bit.ly/SMYH1u

Acknowledgements

I would like to thank the following people:

Michele DeFrance who for years read almost every word I wrote minutes after I'd written it. Her unwavering enthusiasm for my writing has been so heartening.

Kristin Brown who is a fountain of information about Loudoun County and almost everything else. She was always willing to hash out a plot point when I couldn't get it sorted on my own.

Detective Doug Shaw of Leesburg Police Department. Everything I got right was because of him and anything I might have gotten wrong was entirely my fault.

My cousin, Marty Chapman, who answered many of my questions about police departments in general.

Miller Consulting Group, Inc, who taught me everything I know about private investigation.

My mother, Sarah Crumpton, who has always been so supportive of my writing and keeps my extended family informed.

My sisters, Joan Dier and Julie Goyette, for reading early drafts and offering useful suggestions.

Jennifer Stevens who did a lot of heavy lifting on this book.

Sara Gardiner who makes content edits seem like an ego boost.

Kelly Reed who makes line edits actually fun with his side comments.

Lynn McNamee who saw something I wasn't sure was there.

I'm blessed with an enormous family and many friends all of whom, in one way or another, have made this book possible. Thanks to you all.

About the Author

Marie Flanigan grew up all over the Commonwealth of Virginia as the youngest of three girls. Star Wars and comic books dominated her youth. She has a couple of degrees from George Mason University and is a licensed Private Investigator. Over the years, she's been a disc jockey, a web developer, and a children's librarian.

An avid gamer, she reviews video games for GameIndustry.com. After nine car accidents, five concussions, and brain surgery, she decided that perhaps she was more suited to a quieter life. She and her husband and three dogs live happily and somewhat chaotically outside of Washington DC.

Read more at https://mflanigan.com/.

22721128R00131

Made in the USA
Columbia, SC
01 August 2018